Advance]
Dream

Dream Lover

Dream Lover
Jane Futcher

alyson
books
LOS ANGELES • NEW YORK

Manufactured in the United States of America.
Printed on acid-free paper.

This trade paperback original is published by Alyson Publications Inc.,
P.O. Box 4371, Los Angeles, California 90078-4371.
Distribution in the United Kingdom by Turnaround Publisher Services Ltd.,
Unit 3 Olympia Trading Estate, Coburg Road, Wood Green,
London N22 6TZ, England.

First edition: June 1997

01 00 99 98 97   10 9 8 7 6 5 4 3 2 1

ISBN 1-55583-375-6

Library of Congress Cataloging-in-Publication Data
Futcher, Jane.
    Dream lover / Jane Futcher. — 1st ed.
    ISBN 1-55583-375-6 (pbk)
    1. Lesbians—California—Marin County—Fiction. I. Title.
PS3556.U8D74 1997   97-5004
813'.54—dc21   CIP

Credits
"The Song of Wandering Aengus" reprinted with the permission of Simon &
Schuster from *The Collected Works of W.B. Yeats, Volume 1: The Poems,*
revised and edited by Richard J. Finneran (New York: Macmillan, 1989).

Cover design by B. Zinda.

For Marny Hall

Acknowledgments

It takes a village to raise a novel. I would like to thank all the villagers who coaxed, prodded, and pushed this book into being.

Cleo Jones and Beth Jacobs from my Berkeley writers' group listened with patience, encouragement, and kindness to early drafts of this novel and to the impassioned accounts of the events that inspired it.

My beloved friend Catherine Hopkins, who died on January 4, 1996, introduced me to her special childhood haunts on Long Island's North Shore and read this manuscript in doctors' offices as she awaited tests results and chemotherapy. She and her partner, Joan Alden, held my hand in the darkest times, offering me and my book the kind of unswerving support that most authors dream of and some are lucky enough to get.

My father, Palmer Futcher, has been there since 1947.

Linnea Due spent hours with my characters, generously lending her novelist's eyes and ears and editor's scalpel.

Helen Eisenbach, my first editor at Alyson, gave me hope, a contract, and keen vision. Alyson's Julie K. Trevelyan, Gerry Kroll, Greg Constante, Bob Underwood, and Elaine

Rathgeber have provided their extensive publishing know-how and insight.

Doug Schmidt, Steve Martin, Nanette Gartrell, Dee Mosbacher, Sarah Jane Doyle, David Lebe, Ruffin Cooper, Debi Mazor, Linda Belden, Janie Spahr, Annie Lamott, Dionne Somers, Susan Kennedy, Anne Santos Paxson, and Peggy Kent offered their friendship when it counted.

My cousin Anne Rightor Thornton cried when I stumbled and caught me when I fell.

My friend Marny Hall always seems to understand.

Erin Carney, my lover, partner, friend, and muse, picks me up and makes me laugh.

To all of you, my villagers, I offer my deepest thanks and love.

A friend of mine used to say, "Give us stories. Lesbians need to tell their stories."

Here is my story.

Jane Futcher
Novato, California

□ **Part I** □

Chapter 1

In the moonlight Kate wound up the mountain behind the town of Mill Valley on a rutted road that smelled of sage and blackberries and dust. She had never been on this part of the mountain, silent and unspoiled, where dark shapes of redwoods towered above her. For a moment the fleeting image of a girl running down a green field distracted her. Now, it appeared, she was lost.

Her shift at the spa — four men in a row, including the enormous bearded Sikh who always gave good tips — had exhausted her. *There has to be an easier way to earn $16.50 an hour,* she thought, though most of the time she liked the sensual, impersonal contact. Massage helped Kate's painting, imprinted on her hands a knowledge of the body and the psyche that she was able to translate into her portraits. There were other benefits: the flexible hours, the odd assortment of masseuses who hung out between appointments in the lounge eating yogurt, giving neck rubs, trading stories about difficult clients. And working evenings left her daytimes free.

She squinted into the darkness. Why had she agreed to meet Ellie Sereno Webster tonight? The woman Kate hadn't seen in more than twenty years had insisted they meet right away, wouldn't wait until next week, when Kate could have driven down to Turkey Run, the horsey town twenty-five miles south of San Francisco where Ellie lived. "But I'll be in Mill Valley *tonight*," Ellie pleaded, issuing Kate directions to her friends' house.

Kate no longer saw the redwoods above her or the houses built into the hills. The world had gone to green, to the playing fields of her childhood, to the smell of grass and sprinklers, to a late summer night in Forest Hills, New York, in a dimly lit hotel room, where she and the woman she was about to see for the first time since high school lay in bed, breathless and in love. Kate was fifteen; Ellie, eighteen. They had paid cash for the room, written false names in the register, and given in to the physical attraction that had been building between them for months. It had been without a doubt the defining experience of Kate's youth. The next night, riding back to Washington, D.C., on the charter bus after the men's finals of the U.S. Open, she and Ellie had pressed close to each other in the darkness, amazed and electric and longing to touch again.

A week later Ellie left for Vermont to start her freshman year at Bennington. As quickly as she had fallen into Kate's arms in New York, she disappeared, telling Kate never to contact her again. Inflamed, changed, devastated, Kate returned for three more years at Miss Downey's School in McLean, Virginia.

So what was the glamorous siren of Kate's childhood like at forty-one? As a girl she had played on every varsity team, had boyfriends up and down the East Coast, was known for her astounding breasts that the editors of the 1962 Miss Downey's School yearbook, light-years away from feminist consciousness, had dubbed "Cadillac bumpers." Would she be the same?

Wrenching her Honda into reverse, Kate at last spotted two rows of white lights leading up to a horizontal row of brighter lights. At the top of what looked like a UFO landing strip, a spectacular one-level house stretched across the ridge. It was unbelievable, a Hollywood film set on the crest of a hill, the peaks of Mount Tamalpais rising in the west, the lights of Mill Valley and Tiburon and San Francisco Bay to the east. Ellie had found a breathtaking location for their reunion.

Kate parked in a dusty flat below the house and climbed a staircase flanked by drought-resistant lavender, ceanothus, and oleander. As she rapped on an opaque glass door, heart pounding, Kate could feel the bag of sparkling cider beginning to split in her hands.

When the door opened, Kate stared into huge, startled eyes: An enormous black poodle pawed her white pants. "Bad dog, Shebah. Get down." Kate saw the yellow jumpsuit and Mexican sandals first, then the tall, flushed woman, her cheeks tan, her shoulder-length brown hair streaked with blond, her deep blue eyes lined with mascara and fixed on Kate. Collaring the dog, Ellie slammed the door and enveloped Kate in a cloud of expensive perfume. "You found us, Katie. Marvelous. Look great. Just the same. Damn it, Shebah. Get down."

Kate followed her up the stairs, relieved that Ellie was now a mere mortal, a middle-aged woman who was slightly drunk, a little overweight, and very glad to see her. She led Kate into a room of glass and candlelight that extended from the kitchen and dining area, where she stood now, into the living room, where a fire glowed and a grand piano stood dramatically open, accenting the huge expanse of glass. Empty wine bottles, plates, and glasses on the long oak table made Kate feel as if she were arriving in the third act of a play that had begun hours earlier.

A rosy-cheeked woman, blond hair pulled back in a ponytail and horn-rimmed glasses pushed up on her head, pumped her hand. "I'm Hope Ramirez. We saved you dinner." Pointing to a chair, she handed Kate a plate of pink and green — salmon, perhaps, and steamed spinach.

A dark, soft-spoken man in khaki pants and a lime green polo shirt rose to shake her hand. "I'm Raphael." He pressed a switch on the wall, causing something to whir above them, and Kate watched the roof of the house open and disappear into the eaves. Outside, against the black night sky, floodlights shimmered against the smooth surface of a turquoise swimming pool. There was not even a single light between this house and the lone beacon on the western peak of Mount Tamalpais. Kate could not conceal her astonishment.

"Tell us everything about yourself." Ellie cannonballed into the seat on Kate's left, tipping over a wineglass. "Sorry, Hopie. I'm terribly nervous." She dunked her napkin into the pool of wine and twirled a strand of hair around her fingers. "This is most extraordinary, Kate." Ellie fished a cigarette from the pack of Merits on the table. "How long has it been?" she asked lightly.

"Twenty-four years," Kate said, then blushed for knowing exactly how long.

"Kate and I went to school together." Ellie held the cigarette between her fingers.

"I gathered that," Hope said, striking a match and, in a gesture that surprised Kate, lighting Ellie's cigarette. "Do you live here?"

Ellie leaned forward. "You must tell us everything, Katie. What have you been doing for the last twenty-four years?" An emerald the size of a walnut caught the candlelight as Ellie tapped her ashes into a saucer on the table. "Do you see anyone from Miss Downey's? Are you married? What's your life like?"

Kate ran her fingers through her spiked blond hair. How like Ellie to ask so many questions, to assume this air of familiarity, to lean close to Kate, breasts inches from her shoulder. She had always been flirtatious, of course, even with strangers, with the hotel clerk in New York, with other girls at Miss Downey's. Kate smiled. It didn't matter now. Ellie Sereno, now Ellie Webster, had no power over her. "I'm an artist," Kate began.

"Kate's published a book of photographs," Ellie said to Hope, who was riffling through an address book in search of a phone number. "I found it at Kepler's yesterday and spent the afternoon with it. Do you know all those lesbians, Katie?"

Kate swallowed a mouthful of salmon. "They're mostly — "

"I'm married, of course." Ellie's cigarette sizzled as she dropped it into her saucer. "I have three sons and four horses and a swimming pool in Turkey Run."

"And a husband." Hope smiled, dialing her remote phone. "Don't forget that."

"Yes," Ellie said. "And a husband."

Kate had forgotten the trace of New York in Ellie's voice. Although they lived in northern Virginia, her parents, Kate remembered now, had both grown up on Long Island.

"Tell us about your life, Katie. Tell us about that crazy murder trial in New Orleans. I understand you illustrated the story for the Sunday magazine."

Across the table and just to the right, on the far wall, Kate noticed a painting of two men lounging by a swimming pool in the bright California sun. "Is that — "

"Our other one is on loan to a museum in Minneapolis," Raphael said.

Hope covered the mouthpiece of the phone with her hand. "Milwaukee."

"I've only seen David Hockneys in museums." Kate was thunderstruck. In the living room, above the grand piano, she spied another painting, more abstract, of a cornfield. It was. Shit, yes. A Diebenkorn.

"I'm serious, Kate." Ellie leaned forward on her elbows. "I want to hear about Ginny Foat's trial."

As Kate thought of New Orleans, of Ginny Foat, the president of the California branch of NOW, who had been accused of murdering a businessman, she could not help noticing the cleavage that was visible whenever Ellie leaned forward. Kate glanced at the cider she'd brought, still sitting on the kitchen counter. She needed a drink.

Ellie pushed her hair behind one ear, carelessly tapping her new cigarette into a blue-and-gold Staffordshire dinner plate. "She bludgeoned some man with a tire iron."

"You know her, Kate?" Hope's colossal diamond twinkled in the candlelight.

"Maxine says she's a lesbian," Ellie said almost giddily.

"I thought she was a go-go dancer." Raphael folded his tan arms across his chest. "Father drove a Wonder Bread truck."

"Cocktail waitress," Kate began in a whisper. Instead of relaxing, she was feeling more and more uptight. "There wasn't much evidence. Her husband may have done it. They dragged him out of prison to testify against her. But he wasn't on trial."

Kate remembered the last day of the trial, across the Mississippi River from New Orleans, in the stuffy four-story Metairie courthouse. It was close to Thanksgiving, but the gulf air was hot and clingy. When the jury adjourned to deliberate, forty-odd reporters and court artists fought their way down the corridor for the pay phones, then crowded into the elevator and headed to the catfish café by the levee. Ginny and her lawyers had chosen the same spot. When Kate saw her ashen face, she approached and said softly, "I believe you." A few minutes later the jury had found her not guilty.

"I think she's sexy." Ellie exhaled a puff of smoke.

Kate glanced up at the Hockney, hoping his greens and blues and flat suburban landscape would settle her. Ginny Foat *was* sexy; Kate had always thought so. But why was the married mother of three so intrigued with Foat?

"These photographs of Kate's are incredible," Ellie said. "Some of the women are making love."

Raphael winked at Kate. There was something nice about him, something earthy and amused and unshakable. "Hope went to a girls school in Nevada. More wine?"

"I don't drink." Kate blushed.

"I'll drink yours then." Ellie poured Kate's wine into her own glass, her eyes on Kate. "Hopie's a Hula Hoop heiress."

"Plastics, Ellie." Hope handed Kate a grape Popsicle. "My father manufactured plastic things." She picked up her dessert spoon and tapped it against the long oak table. "Kate, you haven't had a drop of wine. Try some of this chardonnay." She poured Kate a glass from the new bottle, then studied the label. "What do you think? It's a special press from a tiny vineyard in Napa."

"I'm an alcoholic," Kate said finally. "I don't drink."

Hope's smile faded. "That's fabulous."

"What's so fabulous about it?" Raphael had rolled a joint the size of a Cuban cigar. Licking the seam, he lit the cigarette and handed it to Hope, who inhaled deeply.

"I think it's very good that she doesn't drink. My mother's an alcoholic." Hope began coughing violently. She wiped tears out of her eyes and passed the joint to Ellie.

Suddenly Ellie's chair screeched across the tile floor. "Kate, I want you to come to my house for the Fourth of July." She grabbed Kate's arm. "We'll have a barbecue. Hope and Raphael will come too, and we'll go to the children's rodeo in Turkey Run."

What am I doing here? Kate stared through the open roof. Ellie seemed so different from the girl she remembered. So spacey and out of focus.

The swimming pool filter chugged in the silence. "You're all coming?" Ellie looked at each of them.

"The Haases said something about their camp in Idaho," Hope said mildly. "If their plane's not fixed, we'd love to come."

"What about you, Kate?"

Kate longed to be back in her quiet cottage in Sausalito. "I can't."

Ellie's face tightened. "Why not?"

"I paint on weekends. It's the only time I don't work at the spa."

"But it's a holiday. You can't paint on the holiday."

"Paint the rodeo," Hope offered. "It's a visual treat. Kids and cowboys and suburban mothers in their Jeep Wranglers and ten-gallon hats."

"Promise you'll come?"

Kate stood up. "I'm afraid I've got to go."

"You can't leave until you've had a tour." Holding Kate's hand, Ellie led her out of the sliding glass doors onto a terrace. The turquoise swimming pool cantilevered gracefully above the edge of the cliff; to the right was a smaller house perpendicular to the big house.

"That's where Hope and I sleep," Raphael said to Kate. "Ellie too when we're lucky."

"Raphael, please," Hope warned.

"Stay tonight, Ellie," Raphael murmured. "With Kate, if you'd like."

Did they think Kate would do anything just because she was a lesbian? "I've really got to go."

"I'll leave with you." Ellie guided Kate through the house to her car outside. "Good-bye, my darling. I'll call you." She kissed Kate on the lips, leaped into her car, and roared down the hill.

"Come back and swim. Anytime." Raphael also kissed Kate's lips.

Glancing behind her at the glass house, Kate turned down the road and felt the suburbs close in again — the wooden parking decks, the garbage cans out for the morning pickup.

At the Highlife Saloon on Miller Avenue, Kate slowed, then stopped. Ellie Sereno was standing at the corner, leaning against the side of her car, hands dug into her jumpsuit pockets.

"I waited for you," she called.

Kate lowered the window as Ellie leaned down to speak. "I want you to come down to my house tonight. My kids and husband are away. We can ride in the morning. It's perfect."

Kate stared at Ellie's blue eyes and the seductive lean of her torso. "I can't."

Two men in jeans and plaid shirts stumbled out of the saloon. "It almost never happens — everyone away. The house empty."

"Ellie…"

"When I saw your book yesterday, I had so many questions. The pictures moved me."

Why hadn't Ellie asked her questions at dinner? Or if she'd wanted to really talk, why had she insisted on dinner at Hope and Raphael's? "What questions?" Kate said finally.

"Do you have a lover?"

"What?"

"Is there anyone who..."

The thought of Gina infused Kate with a hunger she'd been fighting for weeks to contain. She remembered their last night, turning to see Gina coming toward her naked. They'd made love and afterward ate steamed clams at the seafood place on the water with a chattering fire and Tracy Chapman moaning from the speakers.

"Come home with me tonight."

Ellie's voice startled her. "Thank you, Ellie. I can't."

"May I call you?" Her face was serious, for a moment almost as pure as it had been at eighteen.

"Sure." Ellie's breasts were inches from her own, her perfume almost drowning Kate.

"Why don't you come tonight?"

"Because it's late, and I need to paint, and I have a show in October."

"I won't hold you captive."

The two men from the Highlife were coming toward them. Ellie opened the door of her black car. "Be forewarned then. I'm going to call."

"Okay."

Kate followed Ellie onto the freeway, exiting at Sausalito as the red taillights of the Land Rover disappeared over the hill toward the Golden Gate Bridge and San Francisco.

"I'm afraid I'll go back to the life," Gina had said that last night as they stood by her car near the restaurant. Gina's mocha skin had looked pale, ghostlike.

"I love you."

Gina brushed away a tear. "But when I'm with you, I want to make love with you, and when I make love with you, I have the flashbacks. And the flashbacks make me want to drink, and when I drink, I want to go back to the life. It's so much easier. It's such easy money." Gina was crying.

Kate's body hurt; her ears began to ring. "But we've had such a wonderful evening. How can you say it's over?"

"I'm sorry." Gina backed out of the parking lot.

That was six months ago. Kate descended the hill, smelling the honeysuckle and jasmine from the high Sausalito hedges and the salt from the bay below. She pulled her car into the garage beneath her cottage, relieved to be home. *What if I do see Ellie Sereno again?* she thought, a familiar sadness tugging at her chest. *It could help me forget.*

Chapter **2**

The telephone blared through Kate's small studio. She tried to sound alert.

"Morning," Stacey said.

Kate glanced at the clock. "It's 7 o'clock."

"Should I call you back?"

"Talk to me while I make coffee." Kate glanced at her easel in the corner, where Gina lay dreamily in the hammock portrait, then down at the boats in the marina below. In her tiny kitchen she put water on to boil.

"Where were you last night? I kept calling."

Kate studied the blue water of the bay and the three Hollywood palm trees sprouting out of the little artificial island beyond the marina. A fishing trawler crawled past the island followed by a two-person scull and a fleet of windsurfers. "I went to see my friend from high school. Remember? I told you."

"That's right. My God. The beautiful married hockey player. How was she?"

Kate poured coffee into the filter paper. "I'm not sure."

"Is she still sexy?" Stacey, a novelist, adored any kind of gossip or intrigue.

"I met her at this glass house on top of Mount Tamalpais. Twenty-two acres, no houses, nothing anywhere in sight except the mountain. Her friends have two Hockneys and a Diebenkorn." Kate sipped her coffee. The day would be hot, perfect for painting. "The roof of their house comes off."

"What's she like?"

Kate remembered the endless green playing fields at Miss Downey's, the brown shingled buildings, the paddocks and barns, the pain and secrecy, the intoxicating euphoria of forbidden love. "I'm not sure. Friendly, I guess."

"What's she look like?"

Kate saw the yellow jumpsuit and the blue eyes and the black Land Rover stopped by the Highlife Saloon. "They were all kind of drunk when I got there."

"Oh?" She could hear Stacey's disapproval.

"Not falling-down drunk."

"Were you tempted?" Kate had met Stacey at an AA meeting in San Francisco three years ago, when Kate was newly sober and Stacey, with two years of sobriety and a whimsical sense of humor, had agreed to be her sponsor. They had finished the Twelve Steps ages ago, but their friendship continued strong.

"I was tempted. A little. It was very tense. They live in a different world."

"Very straight?"

"And very rich. The wife is a Hula Hoop heiress."

"Very funny, Katie," Stacey laughed. "Did you talk about the past and what happened between you?"

"No. That's why it was so odd." Kate and Ellie couldn't have been the only girls in love at Miss Downey's, but those feelings were never discussed. Crushes were accepted, but sex was out of the question. "This couple, Raphael and Hope, asked us both to spend the night." She noticed a wisp of smoke rising from the green ridge above the Strawberry Peninsula across Richardson Bay. "Does that seem odd?"

"Very. Was she anything like she was in high school?"

Kate remembered the black dog and the smell of Ellie's perfume and then the feel of her in New York, in the hotel, liquid and dreamy. "On my way home I found her standing out in the road in Mill Valley next to her car. She wanted me to go back with her to Turkey Run, said it was perfect because her husband and kids were away and we could go riding in the morning."

"And you didn't go? What an opportunity!"

"This is my life, not a novel." Kate stared at the Gina painting. Did her mouth seem too angry? Combative? "And I don't know her anymore. She kept saying she really wanted to talk about my work and stuff, but she never did."

"She wants to talk about being a lesbian. They always do. Because of your book."

"Gina was looking for me in a dream I had last night," Kate said suddenly. "She wanted me to come back."

"Katie," Stacey began slowly. "I know you love her, but you're better off without her. She's damaged. Badly."

Kate stood up. Was it the coffee that was making her feel so nervous and strange?

"Were you attracted to Ellie at all?"

"The affair at school traumatized me for years. I thought she really cared about me."

"I'm sure she did. But it was 1962. She was scared."

"I was too."

"Of course you were. But I'll bet she's thought about you as much as you've thought about her over the years. Lunch at Pano's if I'm wrong."

"She was so outstanding at school," Kate said slowly. "This athletic, sort of unapproachable goddess."

"And now she's middle-aged, like the rest of us. I think you should see her again."

Kate swallowed.

"It would be a diversion. Something to take your mind off Gina."

"Out of the frying pan, into the fire," Kate laughed.

"Doesn't have to be. Talk to her. Have lunch with her. Find out what happened. And whatever you do, don't pick up a drink."

Kate dressed in the tiny alcove that had once been the woodshed and was now her bedroom. Since she'd given up her office space on Bridgeway and moved her studio into the cottage, the little house had shrunk. There was not enough room for anything. Still, though she missed the income from free-lance illustration, she did not miss the long hours, the deadlines, the art directors who wanted eleventh-hour changes to please this or that editor or salesperson or publisher. Now Kate was free. She was painting again, making enough from her massage practice and the occasional sale of a photograph to survive. She wondered now, as she put her bag of massage oils and New Age music tapes and pillowcases into the closet, if Ellie Sereno, with her big black Land Rover and horses and husband, ever worried whether she'd have enough money to pay the rent.

The hammock painting of Gina, long legs extended languidly over the rope cords, breasts pressed against her leotard, leather miniskirt climbing her thighs, was going to be very good. Her face was angular, her skin a light, creamy mocha.

Kate remembered the first time she met Gina, when she'd been commissioned to do a picture-story on women who work in San Francisco massage parlors. On the surface the place was remarkably like her own spa in Mill Valley, only the "masseuses" were far more glamorous. Kate had talked with the women late into the evening, sketching them as they gossiped between customers, their faces hardening instantly when the men arrived.

Kate had been sketching the drop-dead-beautiful African-American woman when an elderly, red-faced man in a pinstriped suit had opened the front door.

"Hi, Artie." Gina had disappeared down the carpeted hallway. Twenty minutes later she led the old man to the door, kissed his cheek, then sat down and opened a textbook on accounting, unaffected by whatever had taken place in the small back room. She leaned over Kate's shoulder, tapping her sketch pad. "You like working for the *Chron*?"

Kate shrugged. "I'm freelance, not staff."

"Then they don't own you. When I get my stockbroker's license, I'll work for myself too."

Kate had begun to pack up her pencils and paper.

"Going home?"

"Yep." Kate zipped her portfolio.

"You have a car?"

Kate nodded.

"Mind giving me a lift?"

They made all the lights on Market Street, cruising through the dark, Kate happy, pleased to be gaining some secret knowledge of city life after hours. Gina directed her to a Victorian house off Castro Street.

"Want some coffee?"

Kate hesitated.

"I don't bite."

Gina's place was spacious and modern: white wall-to-wall carpeting, two chrome chairs, a glass table. A sliding door opened onto a deck overlooking San Francisco; there were potted flowers and a hammock strung across one end.

"Do you know the writer?" Gina was grinding coffee.

"Sorry?"

"From the *Chron*?"

"It's a picture-essay."

"Well, whoever writes the captions should know that the trick" — Gina popped some milk into the microwave — "is to get the customer to ask for more. The more they ask for, the more they have to pay."

Kate glanced at Gina's bookshelf: Toni Morrison, a paperback on homeopathic medicine, old copies of *Forbes,* and a textbook on investment strategies. "How do you make them want more?"

Gina slid the tray with coffee onto the floor and handed Kate a cushion. "You touch them in certain places. You know. So they want more."

Kate fought a blush. Gina was disconcertingly beautiful — tall, long-limbed, with a mane of silky black hair and a movie star's perfect features.

"You're shocked." Gina laughed.

"I haven't...been involved with a man in maybe fifteen years."

"Being a lesbian's got nothing to do with it," Gina said quickly. "I'm a lesbian, and I fuck men." Kate inhaled quickly. "Men have boundaries. I can deal with that. Women want your soul." She stopped, abruptly leaning back on one elbow, and pulled gently on Kate's red suspenders. "These are cute." Did she know that her shoulder was touching Kate's breast? "I like artists," Gina whispered, moving closer. She was stroking Kate's hair now, breathing close to her neck. "Good artists, that is."

Kate's heart was pounding. The bed was just a few feet behind them.

"I'm in therapy," Gina said, her hands finding Kate's breasts.

Kate tried to sit up. "I'm sorry?"

"I'm starting to remember my childhood. In West Africa."

"Wow." Kate was suddenly self-conscious.

"My father was a diplomat. Very upright. Very distinguished. He'd sit me on the trunk in the basement and take off his clothes and make me watch him work out with his weights. I remember the sound of his breathing and the peppery smell of his body as he put his dick in my mouth."

Kate buttoned her shirt. "I'm so sorry."

"I don't know you. I can tell you anything."

"I should go home." Kate stood, confused; she shouldn't have come inside. She searched her backpack for her keys.

Gina came closer. "I want to make love with you, Kate," Gina said.

"I really didn't expect — "

"I wanted to touch you when you were drawing me tonight at the spa. I got turned on, seeing you look at me, drawing me. I wanted to do this," she said, taking Kate's hand and lightly kissing the top of it.

Kate swallowed. "I'd better go."

"I can't stop doing the work." Gina's eyes were unfocused and distant now. "I've gotten used to the money."

"I can understand that." Kate opened the door. "Listen, I'm gonna go." She hurried down the stairs into the street.

It was 3 P.M., time to get ready for her shift at the spa. She wished she could keep working on the Gina painting; it was important to take advantage of the intensity. If the painting were truly good, if it showed the soul of her subject — and its creator — it could bring Gina back into her life.

Kate stretched out her legs, grateful for this work. Now, as in childhood, art kept her sane. In her studio she could get to people without talking to them, explore feelings without verbal expression. She could escape the slim, narrow band of acceptable behavior, playing with color and form and narrative to love as she wanted, see as she saw.

She blew out the orange candle on her mantle. One of her massage teachers said you could heal people without touching them. You held your hands over their bodies — close enough to feel their heat and energy — found the tension spots, and redistributed the energy all by moving your hands above the client. Painting was a little like that. When someone sat for a portrait and Kate worked with them, alone, for hours at a time, she saw more than their bodies. As she painted, she entered their bodies psychically, felt their energy, and translated it, subtly altering herself and her subject in the process.

At Miss Downey's, after the affair with Ellie, Kate communicated her love through art but never again through touch. She drew her friends, photographed them, took long walks with them along the Potomac, ate french fries at soda shops.

But never again, not until her senior year of art school in New York, did she touch another girl. What happened with Ellie hurt too much.

Chapter **3**

Kate turned onto the five-lane freeway, heading south for Turkey Run. Three weeks had passed since the strange evening in Mill Valley with Ellie and her friends. Despite the dazzling house and the sexual innuendos, seeing Ellie again — so suburban and even matronly — had been almost anticlimactic. But since that evening something inside Kate had shifted. Kate's energy and concentration increased as she painted. She'd begun a new Gina painting from photographs, a Rousseau-like dream portrait of both of them standing side by side, a jungle of birds-of-paradise, bougainvillea, and tiger lilies closing around them.

When Ellie called, Kate put her off, then finally agreed to have dinner with her in Turkey Run, spend the night, and go riding in the morning. If nothing else, Kate supposed, the evening would be an interesting escape from the studio.

The air cooled as Highway 280 curved around the long blue reservoir at Crystal Springs. Hay-covered pastures replaced the rows of houses of Daly City; the sweet smell of grass, horses, and the country emanated from the far ridges of the Coastal Range mountains. Kate's curiosity about Ellie and her married life increased as she drove. What would Nicky Webster, Ellie's childhood sweetheart, be like after all these years? Would her house be a glass castle like Hope and Raphael's?

On the surface at least, Ellie appeared to have followed most of the rules laid down by Miss Downey and her successors. She had married, had children, lived in a posh suburb of San Francisco. Miss Downey would not have approved of the ménage with Hope and Raphael, if that's what it was, but, on the other hand, Miss Downey allowed the rich and well-connected certain...eccentricities.

Glancing into the rearview mirror, Kate brushed a hand through her spiked hair and wished she did not look so much like she'd spent the last three weeks indoors, which is exactly what she had done. "To be rather than to seem" had been the motto of Miss Downey's School, but in actuality the school's philosophy was the opposite — the appearance of goodness and propriety was at least as important as the real thing. Kate had not lived by all of Miss Downey's rules, but she knew them well. Six years at the school plus six years of ballroom dancing classes and Sunday dinners with her aunts and grandmothers had taught her the cardinal rule of polite society: Keep your deepest feelings under wraps.

Kate obeyed. In seventh grade, when she first met Ellie Sereno, she realized with dismay that she was not "growing out of" her crushes on teachers and upperclassmen, as conventional wisdom suggested she would; her crushes were intensifying. In ninth grade, with the arrival of glamorous boarding students from places like New York and California, she struggled hard against her unruly impulses. While her classmates held hands, hugged, and groomed each other as unself-consciously as gorillas, Kate remained apart. An act as neutral as sharing a hymnal with her seatmate, Claire, at morning prayers made her hands sweat and heart race. More intimate contact was out of the question. As far as she knew, no girl in the history of Miss Downey's School, perhaps even the world, had such attractions. And then came the weekend in New York with Ellie.

As different as they seemed now, she and Ellie had had some things in common. They were both day students, both good athletes, both artistic. Kate's love was painting; Ellie's, music. They waited in the same parking lot for their car pools, attended the same stuffy ballroom dancing school in Georgetown, served on the board of the school literary magazine. But the three-year difference in their ages was a chasm they never crossed until New York.

Kate's heart raced as she entered the postcard-perfect cowboy town of Turkey Run, which she'd illustrated years ago for a story on Bay Area riding stables. Many of San Francisco's wealthiest families had built summer homes here after the earthquake of 1906 and had later escaped there to avoid San Francisco's cold, foggy summers. Today the town looked like a carefully crafted stage set from the Wild West. The local bar had swinging saloon doors; the Wells Fargo bank belonged in *Gunsmoke*. At the hitching posts by Edward's Store, the rarefied grocery patronized by former debutantes and horse trainers, barefoot adolescent girls straddled their horses, sipping Diet Pepsi.

On the trail flanking the road, Kate watched a teenage boy, a dead ringer for Dylan on *Beverly Hills 90210,* rein in an enormous Thoroughbred; a palomino bearing a woman in full rodeo gear came from the opposite direction. A mile beyond the town, beneath the lush overhang of oaks and bay laurels, Kate ascended, passing horse barns and long drives that led to hidden houses. At the top of the hill, paddocks bordered both sides of the road. On the left a low red-shingled ranch house stood at the top of a fence-lined driveway, framed by a flower bed of marguerites, daisies, purple asters, lavender, and orange nasturtium.

Kate was surprised to see several cars in the driveway. Ellie hadn't mentioned any other guests, said it would just be them. Were her flip-flops, jeans, and blue-striped jersey nice enough?

"Hello?" Kate stood on the brick steps in front of the open door.

Dotty Henry, the blond bouncy cheerleader from Kate's class at Miss Downey's, hugged her. "Hey, Katie. You know Charles, my husband." She introduced a man as blond and cheerful as she was. "Ferguson, Andy, say hello to Kate Paine." Two cheerful five-year-old boys in sailor suits dutifully extended their hands.

Kate turned. Ellie kissed her on the lips and looked inside her paper bag. "Diet Cokes. How divine! Kate doesn't drink," she said to Dotty. "Isn't that wonderful?"

"Super," said Dotty.

"What can I get you?" Ellie was wearing a jumpsuit, this time an orange one, and her Mexican sandals.

"You didn't tell me this was a party," Kate whispered.

"It's not a party. It's a Miss Downey's reunion."

Kate rubbed her forehead, aware now that until she talked privately with Ellie about what had happened years ago, she would feel uneasy in her presence. A tall man in khaki pants and a pink Brooks Brothers' shirt came out of the kitchen holding a bottle of red wine. His graying hair was swept back off his head and slicked down in a European, sort of Claus von Bulow way. No doubt about it. This was Nicky Webster, the former crew star from Saint Paul's and Yale.

"Nickers," Ellie said, "do you know Kate Paine? From Dotty and Claire's class at Miss Downey's."

"Pleased to meet you." He pumped Kate's hand warmly. "Would you like some wine?"

"Thanks. I'll have a Coke." Kate took a seat in front of the fireplace, across from the blond family on the sofa. The house was furnished simply — wicker chairs and sofa, brass lamps, and a few antique chairs that looked like they might have belonged to somebody's great-aunt. Redwood beams stained dusty white stretched across the ceiling. Above the fireplace was a stuffed tropical bird frozen in a dramatic, predatory pose with wings outstretched.

Ellie saw her staring. "That's Pilar, our cockatoo. Nicky had him stuffed."

"He looks dangerous." Kate pinched one of his talons.

"I know. The taxidermist misrepresented his personality. He was utterly adorable. His only words were 'I love you.' " Ellie mimicked the bird's funny lisp. "My son Simon let him out one Sunday, and he flew up into the redwood tree by the barn and wouldn't come down. We tried everything. Even had the fire department. He just sat there for days saying 'I love you' until he starved to death and fell to the ground." Kate found herself laughing at the macabre story. Ellie was still very funny.

"Ellie? Nicky?" Claire and Jamie Ramsay were at the door. Kate was glad. Claire had been her seatmate for two years at Miss Downey's. They rarely saw each other in San Francisco, though Claire made a point of coming to Kate's shows and every now and then invited Kate to one of her fancy San Francisco dinner parties. Claire was an attorney, had huge brown eyes, and was dangerously thin; Jamie owned radio stations.

"Thank God, you're here," Claire said, pulling Kate into a bedroom off the living room. "We never know what to expect at Ellie and Nick's."

"Why?" Kate followed behind her.

"They're both a little" — Claire puckered her lips in the mirror — "unpredictable. Nicky's latest enterprise is a crystal mine in Arkansas. Keeps wanting Jamie to invest in it. It makes no sense, and he's exhausted his trust fund trying to make it work." Claire sat down on the bed. "Which is too bad for Ellie. They live on a shoestring." Having four horses and a house in Turkey Run was not the kind of shoestring Kate was used to. "And you know how Ellie is."

"I really don't." Kate searched for the source of the children's music she heard playing in the distance. "I haven't seen Ellie since Miss Downey's."

"Well, she's exactly the same."

"But what was she like then?"

"You knew her better than I did," Claire smiled, squinting at a cracked tile in the bathroom floor. "She's a party girl. Likes to have a good time. I love the fact that she and Nicky smoke pot." It always surprised Kate that her old friend, an ambitious, high-achieving San Francisco socialite, loved nothing better than to get stoned and listen to the Grateful Dead.

A child's laughing voice seemed to come from the door next to the bathroom. Claire removed a joint from her pocket, lit it, inhaled, held her breath, offered it to Kate, who declined, then rubbed it out in the sink. "Ellie's," she exhaled, "larger than life. I can't explain. You know about the little boy, don't you?" She pointed to a photograph on Ellie's dresser, a snapshot of a skinny smiling child of about six, ready to dive into a swimming pool. "He's retarded, I think. It's terribly sad. She puts him away when company comes."

Kate glanced at the room off the bathroom. The little boy was in there, she realized, listening to music tapes.

"We only see them once a year at the most." Claire headed for the door. "I'm totally starved. Ellie doesn't have any help. Insists on these *picnics*. I hope we don't have to wait for hours. I'm trying not to drink."

Ellie offered no food, and Nicky poured more wine, lecturing them good-naturedly on the business of harvesting and selling crystals.

Without warning, Ellie jumped up, pulled the little boys off the sofa, and announced she was taking them riding.

"Now?" Claire pushed her black Dior jacket up her thin arms.

"Come with me, Kate," Ellie said. "Help me saddle up."

Kate knew nothing about horses, but getting outside in the fresh air might help relieve this tension. She watched Ellie expertly saddle a calm red quarter horse named Monkey, leading him across the road to a ring where Dotty and her boys were waiting. The view was tremendous: San Francisco Bay before them, the mountains behind, the sun just now dropping in the west.

Ellie hoisted the younger boy up on the red horse, guiding him around the ring in her bare feet. As Kate watched she was startled to see for the first time a glimpse of the beautiful, fear-less athlete she'd known at school. Ellie trotted alongside the horse, delighting the children, looking young and happy and pure. She was Artemis now, goddess of the untamed wilderness, at ease with her body, at home on the earth. Kate ran to her car for the old Pentax she kept under the seat. She photographed Ellie lengthening the stirrups for the older boy, trotting him around the sandy ring, hoisting up the other child.

"Don't waste your film," Ellie grinned.

Away from the others, Ellie was charming. Kate liked the fact that she wanted the kids to ride, to enjoy their trip to the country more than she cared about feeding the adults.

"Can I help you with dinner?" Dotty called, seeing that Ellie was about to take the younger boy around a second time. It was almost completely dark.

Ellie seemed surprised. "Are you hungry?"

"Very," Dotty said politely. Ellie and the children put away the red horse while Kate returned to the house, which was dark and very cold.

"Where is she?" Claire whispered.

"They're unsaddling the horse."

"Unbelievable." Claire shook her head. "Is she planning to feed us?"

Nicky passed around a hunk of raw crystal as his guests stared dismally into the unlit fireplace.

At 10 P.M. Ellie pulled a roast chicken from the oven, stirred some noodles into a pesto sauce, and dressed the salad. "Dinner," she called, sticking a loaf of warm French bread in a basket. She hadn't needed to shout; all the guests were hovering beside her, plates in hand.

On pillows around the fireplace, the men discussed Jamie's new antique motorcycle. Dotty leaned toward Kate. "Are you doing another book of photographs?"

Kate sliced her chicken. "I'm painting again. Not taking pictures right now."

27

"I bought her book in Palo Alto," Ellie said brightly. "It's fabulous, Dotty. Have you seen it? All women. Some of them are kissing."

Suddenly the room grew silent. Nicky sighed audibly. "I'll show you," Ellie said, disappearing into the bedroom. She returned with the large paperback, holding up the pictures Kate had taken of lesbian couples across the country. The other guests were silent. "Lovely," Dotty said. "Are they…"

"All lesbians," Ellie smiled.

"Your friends?" Dotty asked sweetly.

Before Kate could answer, Nicky steered the conversation away from lesbians to Jamie's new transmitter, then to Maine, where Ellie's parents owned a house, and on to the price of real estate in the Ozarks. The women pored over the book. "Oh, God," Ellie leaped up. "The dessert's on fire." Kate watched her pull two pies, black and smoldering, from the oven.

Jamie stood above Kate, offering her his hand. "Let's play Ping-Pong." On the terrace, by the swimming pool, they slapped the little white ball across the low green net. Just doing something made Kate feel better.

Ellie approached, eating pie with her fingers. "I'll play the winner." She winked at Kate.

Kate accepted the dare. Spinning the ball into the corners, she surprised Jamie by beating him with drop shots and backhands that pulled him out of position. "Your turn, Ellie," he surrendered.

In the half-light by the pool, Ellie and Kate rallied. How many times, Kate wondered, had she watched Ellie play hockey, basketball, tennis, admired and cheered the athlete with the drop-dead body? Now here they were, two middle-aged women who had loved each other as girls, meeting again at a Ping-Pong table. It was the first honest moment she had had with Ellie since their meeting three weeks ago. As they began to play in earnest, their small talk stopped. Kate felt an unbearable tension building in her chest; she was fourteen, on the field, close to Ellie Sereno, feeling that longing, wanting Ellie Sereno to notice her. Kate hoped the others couldn't see how nervous she had become, couldn't hear her heart pounding.

As Kate looked up, Jamie snapped their picture with Kate's camera. Ellie took the lead. Kate caught up, smashing a shot to the corner of the table that bounced wildly, out of Ellie's reach, into the swimming pool.

"You win," Ellie cried. The dinner guests clapped as she put down her paddle, wrapping an arm around Kate's waist.

The sudden warmth of Ellie's touch sent a jolt through Kate's legs.

"You should play Ping-Pong more often, Ellie," Nicky said, patting Ellie's back. "You look happier than I've seen you in ages." Jamie took their picture. Ellie drew Kate closer. Nicky poured more wine.

"I only lost because I'm drunk." Ellie pushed her bangs from her face. "Who wants coffee?"

The others had had enough; in minutes the living room was empty. At the front door Nicky extended his hand to Kate. "Nice meeting you." He'd forgotten her name.

Kate swallowed. "Actually, I think I'm staying here tonight."

Nicky glanced at Ellie, who was clearing glasses from the living room. "Kate's riding with me in the morning," she said coolly.

His hopeful expression changed. "Well, I'm going to bed."

"You might at least help clean up the — "

"Do it in the morning," he said, loosening his tie. "Too tired now."

"Too drunk now," Ellie hissed to his retreating back.

Chapter 4

In silence the women cleared the dishes, washed pots and pans, and loaded the dishwasher, which now hummed by the sink. Ellie brought the candles in from the living room, poured herself another glass of wine, turned off the overhead light, and sat down at the kitchen table as Kate eyed the bottle of wine there. No, she thought, I will live through this without a drink.

Ellie dipped an unlit cigarette into the flame. "Thank God that's over," she said, winking at Kate. "I've been looking forward to this moment since I found your book at Kepler's."

Kate smiled uncertainly.

Ellie drew in on her cigarette, calmer, more real now. "So, Dotty Henry tells me that you brought your lover to the Miss Downey's 15th reunion. What was that like?"

Kate tipped back in her chair and sipped her cold coffee. Stacey was right: Ellie wanted to talk about her sexuality.

"I was still drinking then," Kate shrugged. "At the time I thought I was educating my classmates. I shocked a few people, but I don't think I made much of an impact."

"Word got around." Ellie twisted a gold band around her wedding finger. "I thought it was extremely brave."

"Alcoholic stupor," Kate smiled, telling Ellie about the class dinner in McLean at the house of Sandy Van Slyck, whose father had raised Kentucky Derby winners. They'd served some powerful tequila sunrises, and Emily, Kate's lover, had whispered to her that one of the husbands, a Washington boy, Senator Devereux's grandson, had tried to grope her in the study. Kate and Emily escaped into the garden, green and lush after a light spring rain, and circled back behind the duck pond, hand in hand. The next day Kate's friend Rosie got a call from Ellen Brown, who said that the Van Slyck's gardener had told the McKenzie's cook, who'd told Mrs. McKenzie, who'd spread the word that Kate had been holding hands with her lesbian lover.

Ellie hooted. "I can see those girls and their husbands sipping their cocktails, dissecting every detail. Especially the men — old Alex McKenzie and Sandy Van Slyck. Why are so many men turned on by two women making love?"

Kate felt something inside her relax. They were finally talking honestly.

Ellie lit another cigarette. "When I was pregnant with Simon — " She paused. "I fell in love with a woman. We were lovers for five years."

Kate felt her new calm slip away. Ellie had been leading up to this since she'd first called Kate three weeks ago. Was it true then that the siren of her youth was still a lesbian, had been living a lie all these years?

"When you were pregnant?" was all Kate could think to say.

"I was twenty-six." Ellie's blue eyes were no longer clouded by wine and boredom and smoke.

Kate's heart was pounding.

"I've always lived a double life." Ellie cocked her head to the side. "Margo and Nicky and I would go down to jazz clubs in the Village, snort cocaine till 2 A.M., have breakfast at the Brasserie. Margo had a co-op across the street from us. She'd come back in the morning after Nicky went to work, when the

31

children were in the park with their nurse. We'd make wild, passionate love for hours."

Stacey would love this. A lesbian debauch amid ruling-class splendor.

Ellie stared into the flame. "We had a brownstone on East 69th Street and a house in Southampton. We thought we were gods."

Kate visualized Ellie's deck in the Hamptons, potted geraniums, canvas chairs, endless icy vodka and sunshine, Ellie eating caviar and hard-boiled eggs with her husband and female lover. *She's a lesbian. She's as queer as I am,* Kate kept thinking, relieved but angry.

"That's why when I saw your photographs, I wanted to talk to you so much. You're so open about who you are."

She and Ellie must have lived in New York at the same time, Kate realized. While Kate was working in the Doubleday bullpen, designing book jackets for $150 a week, living in the Village with Liz and marching down Seventh Avenue in gay pride parades, Ellie was snorting cocaine with her café society friends in the Hamptons. "Do you still see her? Your lover?"

"She lives in Santa Fe. Hated me for years, even after we'd broken up and she was happily living with her new lover. She felt I should either leave Nicky and become a lesbian or stay with him and behave myself." Ellie's eyes seemed to ask for Kate's approval. "But I had two children and no money. I wasn't free."

Kate pulled her sweater around her. Ellie had never let go of the good life, the privileges of her class and marriage. "Some things don't change."

"What?"

"Some things don't change," Kate repeated.

Ellie seemed not to hear. "I wish I'd known you then."

Kate shook her head. "I was too queer for you. I wouldn't have fit into your double life."

"You're being sarcastic." Ellie tilted back in her chair. "Margo and I were actually very happy with our double life in the beginning. She thoroughly intended to get married. It wasn't until she realized that she didn't want a husband that things got complicated." Ellie's eyes seemed to measure Kate's reaction. "She wanted me to leave Nicky."

"I can understand that," Kate said dryly.

"But how could I? I couldn't have supported myself. I didn't know how to *do* anything."

"Didn't Margo have money?"

"Oodles. But we weren't like you, Katie. We wanted to have sex, but we didn't want to be lesbians. We had so much," she said wistfully.

"But it was based on a lie," Kate said softly.

"What blew me away was the sex. The intimacy. The closeness. I'd never felt anything like that before."

"You hadn't?" Kate said, angry again. A moth bounced against the plate glass outside. Kate rubbed her hands together, feeling the chill of this house.

"Why are you angry?"

Kate inhaled. *Go ahead. Tell her now,* she thought. *Get it over with.* "Have you forgotten, Ellie? Have you put it out of your mind so completely?"

"What?" Ellie said, looking hurt and confused.

"We were lovers, you and I. In New York. That weekend changed the course of my life. You *had* felt that kind of intimacy before. With me."

"You mean Forest Hills?" she said tentatively.

"Yes!" Kate shot back. "You were as blown away by it as I was. And then you left for Bennington and told me never to contact you again. And now you talk to me about your feelings for Margo as if I should be surprised."

"I'm sorry." Ellie propped her jaw on the palm of her hand and closed her eyes.

"Did you really forget, Ellie?" Kate was incredulous.

There was another long silence. The rinse cycle of the dishwasher clicked off.

"I remember parts of it. The hotel. Feeling very close to you." Ellie reached for Kate's hand.

Kate pulled it away. "Then explain to me why you ran away. I can't be your friend, can't take you seriously until you tell me." The dishwasher hummed in the far corner.

Ellie's face changed from bright to pensive. She leaned forward on her elbows. "It could never have worked, Katie. You were fifteen, and I was a freshman in college."

"Of course it couldn't have worked. That's not what I'm asking."

"What are you asking?"

"Why you cut me off. I was fifteen years old. What you did hurt terribly." Kate swallowed, remembering her shame, her longing to tell someone what had happened. "What confused me so much was that I thought you cared about me. You told me you loved me."

"Did I?" Ellie said, looking down.

"You don't remember?" Denial was a powerful force. Kate knew that. But still.

Ellie touched Kate's hand. "I was crazy about you."

"Thank you," Kate said. She exhaled. Her neck and shoulders had become like vises.

"But I wanted to be normal."

"I believe that." Kate took another breath, her body relaxing. "What's so sad is that you *were* normal. We were both normal. We were attracted to each other, that was all."

Ellie stared down at the table.

Kate leaned forward.

Ellie bit her lip and looked up. "I want so much for us to be friends, Katie." Her eyes reached for Kate's.

Kate swallowed. "After Forest Hills I went sort of crazy. I was afraid to be close to anybody. So it's painful to hear about Margo and your fast-lane life when you've never acknowledged our relationship or explained why you ran away."

Ellie rubbed her eyes. "It's hard to remember what I felt at the time."

"You remember what you felt for Margo."

"I was an adult then. You and I were kids. We were lovers for a weekend. And I did what I always do."

"Which was?"

Ellie looked away at the photograph of two Arabian horses on a calendar pinned to the wall. "It sounds so awful."

"I want to know."

"If something looks hopeless, I cut it off."

"Cut it off?" Kate shivered.

Ellie looked thoughtful. "I've always had the ability to move on without looking back. Especially in those days, when I was utterly impulsive and selfish."

"And you're not now?" Kate's tone was cold.

"Not the way I was with you and then with Margo. I thought I was invulnerable. I thought I could do anything and get away with it — physical danger, sports, drugs, love affairs, whatever. The riskier, the better." Ellie tapped her cigarette. "And then I had Nathan." She looked up at Kate. "I've told you about Nathan, haven't I?"

Kate shook her head. "Claire said something."

"What did Claire say?"

"That he's — "

"Brain-damaged." Ellie inhaled on her cigarette. "He's not as smart as a dog." She glanced at a child's scribbled drawing on the cupboard. "Nathan taught me what it means to really love someone. All my relationships before that — all my affairs and my marriage — were something else." Ellie leaned back in her chair. "I probably love him because he's the child who's most like me."

"In what way?" Kate asked, feeling for the first time that perhaps there was a person occupying the body of Ellie Webster.

She picked up a pack of matches and put them down again. There was a long silence in which Kate heard a dog barking down on the road. "Part of me has always thought that if I had one more woman, one really terrific blowout of an affair, I'd get the whole woman thing out of my system." She wound the cellophane seal from her cigarettes around her finger. "I know

35

you must think that's crazy. 'How the hell does she think she's ever going to be happy with her husband?' "

"Something like that," Kate said.

"Men have the power. And I'm not willing to give that up." Ellie stared out the window; there was a light near the paddock. *What if Nicky were to come in the kitchen now?* Kate wondered.

Ellie motioned toward the barn. "The horses are a great aphrodisiac. I meet someone at a party, take her riding, and before long...you know. I've always had someone."

Kate fought a blush. Ellie had invited *her* riding.

"What are you thinking?" Ellie asked.

Kate pushed her chair from the table. "I'm thinking I need to take a walk." Their talk left her body wired and tight. She would never be able to sleep.

"Perfect." Ellie leaped up. "Get your shoes. We'll go for a walk on the ridge."

The moon, full and huge, hung silver over the bay. Beyond the corral where Ellie and the children had ridden, a narrow trail wound north along the ridge through manzanitas and madrones, down narrow ravines, up through the redwoods.

As they walked Kate felt a disarming, nerve-racking closeness to Ellie. *She's still a lesbian,* Kate kept thinking as she walked behind her friend on the narrow path. *She is not a straight married woman. She's queer, hopelessly attracted to women. She's acknowledged our love and her cruelty.*

In the darkness they approached a gate and climbed over it. Ellie squeezed Kate's arm, her breasts brushing Kate's shoulder. "I was desperate to talk to you that night in Mill Valley. I gave this whole silly party just so I could see you again. If you'd only been more cooperative..."

"I thought I was," Kate said grimly. "I didn't know you were having a Miss Downey's reunion."

Something rustled in the brush. Ellie picked up a stone and tossed it into the trees. "You said no so many times, I thought I wasn't enough by myself."

Kate stared at the dark shapes near the path. It was eerie here but lovely beyond words. She felt ignited, overstimulated. Ellie reached back and folded her left hand over Kate's. *Ellie Sereno is holding my hand. The girl I loved as a child is walking under the full moon at my side at 1 a.m. in the California hills, where the rules of the East do not apply.*

Ellie's touch was spinning her back into the past, into the years when she was not allowed, had not allowed herself to touch anyone. As their feet padded along the dry mountain path, Kate heard a voice: *No one will lock me up for this. No one can hurt me now.*

Climbing the gates, smelling the sage and bay laurels, hay and horse manure, hearing the grasshoppers and crickets and frogs, Kate knew she would always remember this warm, moonlit California night.

The woods opened into a pasture.

"There's a pond just down the hill," Ellie said softly. "Would you like to — "

"Yes," Kate said. They descended a red clay path to a small clearing. Kate could feel the pond nearby, hear the frogs splashing in but could not see it in the darkness. As they lay down together in the grass, Kate ricocheted between the girl she'd longed for and the woman beside her.

"Tell me about your lover," Ellie whispered. "The one you're recovering from."

Kate's chest tightened. "What do you want to know?"

"Anything. Everything. How did you meet?"

Kate remembered the mad, wonderful day soon after she'd met Gina at the spa. Gina had called her, proposed a picnic on the cliffs above Sausalito. After, they soaked at the spa on Bridgeway, danced at Clementina's on Folsom Street. Their year together had been passionate, full of changes: Gina had left prostitution, started a job as a broker, begun to heal from the incest with her father; Kate had stopped freelancing and begun painting full-time. "I was illustrating a story for the *Chronicle,*" she said finally. "There's a photograph of her in my book."

"Which one is she?"

"She's lounging on a couch...in a massage parlor."

"Ah," Ellie said. "She was a...prostitute?"

Kate spoke of Gina, but her thoughts were of Ellie, on what it would be like to undress her, unbutton her jumpsuit, her bra, draw her cheek across Ellie's breasts and clavicle. "She *was* a prostitute. She's a stockbroker now."

"You're still upset?" Ellie said softly.

"Yeah." Kate nodded.

"Why did you break up?"

A chorus of crickets sang in the dark. "I don't really know. The last time we saw each other, we were madly in love."

"Strange."

The country air, the sound of animals rustling, the pleasure of feeling Ellie next to her made Kate expansive. "She was molested as a child, and she'd have these flashbacks whenever we made love. She'd decide she couldn't see me, and then we'd have these amazing reunions." Kate bit her lip. "I kept thinking we could work it out. We liked each other so much."

Ellie kissed Kate's hand. "I feel lucky to be here with you tonight."

A shiver ran through Kate's body as the memory of Gina dissolved. "Do you?"

"You're so pure," Ellie whispered. "So honest about your life, about who you are."

Kate saw herself at school in her gym tunic, stiff, hiding, longing to express the feelings she denied. "When we were kids, you were a goddess to me. You know that. You belonged to another world." She probably shouldn't say these things, but she wanted to be finished with the past, to exorcise it. The only way she knew was to talk about it honestly with the person who affected her so deeply. "I left that world, our world of private schools and country clubs when I came out as a lesbian. I closed that door behind me, and I didn't want to go back. But there was one thing I really missed, one of the only things I missed from all those years in Washington. And that was you."

"Me?"

"You were the first person, man or woman, I ever...touched." The words made Kate feel terribly vulnerable. "I wanted you so much. And that weekend was such a landmark. So hot and sexy and important. I *wanted* you. I wanted to see you again." She forced herself to continue. "And here we are, holding hands under a full moon on a summer night in California."

Ellie's hand tightened on Kate's. Softly she said, "Are our worlds really so different?" The frog chorus grew louder around them.

Kate was floating. "My friends are poor artists."

Ellie's voice went cold. "I'm terrified of being poor."

Kate was not sure how much longer she could fight off this desire, this heat in her legs, this longing to slide down the weightless curve of Ellie's touch.

"One day I'm going to have to choose," Ellie said slowly. "One of these days the other shoe is going to drop."

"Which shoe?" Kate blinked.

"My husband," Ellie said.

Kate had forgotten about Nicky; she wanted to fall and float and talk till dawn with this beautiful woman who was finally telling Kate the truth after 24 years. "Should we go back?"

Ellie rose, extending a hand to Kate, whose legs were shaking from tension and desire. But Ellie — mobilized by guilt or maybe fear — was already moving forward in the darkness.

In the house Ellie opened a door off the kitchen. "This is Simon's room. The boys are at scuba-diving school on Catalina Island." Here, in her son's room, Ellie looked tired and uncertain. The wilderness Amazon was gone. They stood in silence. "I can't tell you what this has meant to me," Ellie whispered.

"And to me," Kate said.

Ellie stepped forward, her lips touching Kate's, her breasts full against Kate's chest. Kate's arms closed around her. But Ellie pulled back. "Nicky will be..." She turned toward the kitchen. "I can't."

"Here," Kate said, taking off the flannel-lined blue-jean jacket Ellie had loaned her. "This is yours." Something about the gesture, the act of undressing, stirred them both. Ellie hesitated, then came forward again and opened her arms. Kate relaxed into them, feeling Ellie's breasts again, feeling both hearts pounding. And then she felt her body tighten, her head throb, her chest tremble, and the tears come.

"Sweetheart, what is it?" Ellie spoke gently.

"Nothing. Everything," Kate sobbed. She could not stop. And Ellie held her, waited, did not pull away.

"Are you so unhappy?" she said at last.

Kate shook her head. She did not want to move, to leave Ellie's arms. It felt so good. "I'm fine. I'm actually really happy. Very, very happy."

Nose running, eyes tearing, Kate pulled away and stared into Ellie's eyes, which were gentle and were blue like her own. "Your eyes are amazing" was all Kate said.

Ellie fingered Kate's collar in a gesture that turned her electric. "You'll be okay?"

"I'll be fine."

Ellie backed out of the room, eyes fastened on Kate, who for the first time noticed Ellie's battered brown cowboy boots.

Chapter **5**

Kate stood in the kitchen doorway as Nicky, Ellie, and Nathan Webster sat eating their breakfast. "Hi," she said self-consciously.

"Good morning," Ellie returned, tired and without last night's warmth. At the table where she and Kate had talked so intimately, Ellie sat, hair uncombed, in thick blue glasses, wrapped in a turquoise bathrobe, scooping oatmeal into the mouth of a skinny blond child in a high chair. Nicky was reading *The Wall Street Journal,* his shirt sleeve splotched with green pesto sauce from dinner.

Kate felt as if she'd awakened from high drama to find herself on *The Donna Reed Show.* Last night she had been riding a tidal wave of emotion, had hovered on the verge of making love to Ellie Webster. Now she was caught in the middle of Ellie's *real* life. *Breathe,* she told herself. *Everything's okay.* She hesitated, then sat down on Ellie's side of the table. As Ellie continued feeding the little boy with the sweet smile, Kate saw that his brown eyes were violently crossed. This was Nathan, then, the retarded son.

"Nathan," Ellie cooed, "can you say hello to Kate? We went to school together. We played *field* hockey together. Isn't that wonderful, my sweetheart?"

Nathan grinned and clapped his hands, which, like his face and bib and the floor around him, were covered in oatmeal. To avoid staring, Kate studied the wisteria vines reaching around the kitchen window as Ellie popped a tape into a red plastic cassette player on the counter. *"And on his farm he had some pigs,"* sang scores of children. *"Ee-eye-ee-eye-oh."* The music assaulted Kate's groggy head. "Have you got any coffee?" she asked.

Ellie's chair yelped against the tile. She yanked a jar of instant coffee from a cupboard, poured some hot water into a mug, and handed it to Kate. "Kate is an artist, my honey lamb," she crooned again, holding a battered silver mug to Nathan's lips. "She takes photographs and paints beautiful pictures. Maybe she'll paint one of you, my Moona Loo."

Nicky spoke without looking up from the paper. "If the consortium gets its financing together, the mine sale is on. I'm talking to their agent today." When no one replied, Kate wondered if he were talking to her. As she formulated a response, a horn honked at the bottom of the driveway.

"Nickers, darling, Nathan's bus is here. Take him down, will you?"

"Haven't finished my breakfast, Lili," he said, still focused on his newspaper.

Ellie stood up. "Nicky, please. I'm not dressed."

Nicky's blue eyes shot daggers at his wife. "You're not dressed because you stayed up half the night." He threw open Nathan's high chair and reached for his son's wrist.

"Nicky, don't be rough with him! And wash his hands." Ellie followed Nicky out the door, dangling a wet washrag. "At least wipe his face."

"For Christ's sake," he snapped. "If you'd come to bed with me at a normal hour, you wouldn't still be undressed."

"He's your son too!" Ellie yelled. Kate sat, listening to their footsteps crunch down the gravel drive. This wasn't *The Donna Reed Show* after all. She wished she could disappear, could be back in her cozy studio. But she was stuck — exhausted and out of place.

"Welcome to a morning in the life of the privileged, Katie." Ellie smiled, dropped the *San Francisco Chronicle* on the kitchen table, and spoke more gently. "I'm afraid I was quite drunk last night."

"The full moon," Kate offered, then wondered why she was giving Ellie an excuse to dismiss the time they'd spent together.

"Exactly. The moon. Are you ready to ride?"

Horses had always scared Kate. "I'm a terrible rider."

"I'll put you on Monkey. You saw how good he was with the kids last night."

"Maybe I'll have a piece of toast," Kate said, thinking it would be cowardly to go home now.

At the barn Ellie clumped across the cement breezeway in her cowboy boots, instructing Kate on how to curry and comb a horse, how to adjust the bridle, how to tighten the girth and lengthen the stirrups, none of which Kate could do correctly because she was calculating the number of minutes she had left to live. She hoped Ellie couldn't see her knees tremble as she mounted Monkey.

"Don't worry, my sweet. You'll learn," Ellie said as if Kate would be riding with her often. They followed the same sandy trail they had traveled in the moonlight, only now they could see the bay to the east and the mountains behind them. Ellie rested her hand on the butt of her lanky brown mare and turned backward to talk. "How you doing? You look great on that horse, Kate. You're a natural."

Kate blushed. "It's different here in the daylight." It was hot and less ethereal now, but riding through the hills, a powerful horse beneath her, rocking her, connecting her to the earth, and the sight of Ellie, her back to Kate, tall in the saddle, excited her. For almost an hour they rode through bay laurels and madrones, passing a white clapboard farmhouse and a pasture where horses grazed, and then down into a cool, dark canyon. They crossed a dry streambed and began to ascend a wide red-clay fire road in the redwoods.

Ellie turned. "Want to go fast?"

Kate swallowed.

"Just hang on to Monkey's mane. Like this."

Before Kate could protest, Ellie grabbed her horse's mane, kicked its withers, and galloped up the dirt road. Kate fell forward, her own horse lurching to catch up with Ellie's. Miraculously Kate stayed on. She was completely out of control, but the motion, the cool air against her cheeks, the red trunks whipping by, and the feeling of the strong animal surging between her legs were amazing. No wonder the horses were Ellie's aphrodisiac. A breakneck run like this through the California redwoods with this feeling of weightless flight and the thud of the pounding hooves would bring anyone back for more.

At the top of the hill, Ellie stopped and grinned. "Did you like that?"

Kate pushed back the straw cowboy hat Ellie had loaned her. "Once I realized I wasn't going to die."

"I wouldn't let you die." Ellie kicked her horse and trotted on, back in the sun again, up another fire road to the top of an open ridge clustered with coastal oaks and bay laurels. A mile below, to the east, was the freeway, but from here they could not hear it. When they came to the hill's crest, they stopped and dismounted, tying the horses to some low branches near the trail. On a sloping field facing the far green ridge to the west, they lay down side by side.

Kate stared up at three turkey buzzards floating above. "Did last night really happen? The talking and the walking?"

Ellie did not answer. Then she said, "Sometimes I despise my husband."

Kate picked a strand of grass and began to chew it. Where their legs touched she could feel her blood pulsing, just as it had in last night's erotic limbo.

"You like riding, don't you? You'll ride with me again."

"Sure," Kate said. "But I'm scared."

"You ride well."

Kate chewed her grass. "It's not just the riding."

"What is it?" Ellie leaned next to Kate, her denim shirt open at the neck. "Was it something I said? Something about last night?"

Kate stared across the valley at the dark tree-covered ridge. This was all so dreamlike. She hated to disturb the reverie by telling Ellie how disturbed she was by the scene at breakfast this morning.

"Do you still," Ellie said in a whisper, "think that something important happened?"

Kate inhaled the smell of this field, of this golden brown hillside, of Ellie's perfume. "I remembered why I fell in love with you," Kate said, afraid to look at Ellie's eyes.

Ellie nodded and kissed Kate's hand. "I've had so many memories. Of that time. Of Forest Hills."

"But you weren't in love with me." Kate felt her neck muscles tighten.

"Wasn't I?" Ellie wiped her eyes with the bottom of her shirt.

Kate squinted into the sun. "You tell me."

Ellie leaned closer. "Your being an artist excites me. That and your honesty."

"Because you're such a liar," Kate grinned.

"That hurts," Ellie said, rolling onto her side away from Kate. "I'm going away next week."

Kate pulled Ellie back so they were facing. "Where?"

"To Long Island, then to Maine. For a month." She said it stoically, as if she were describing a criminal sentence. "It's a chance for my sons to see their grandparents."

"I love Maine," Kate said, remembering the pine-covered islands she'd visited as a girl, the cold salt water, the spare wooden houses, the gulls and lobster pots and granite rocks and lighthouses.

Ellie rubbed her eyes. "Maine is fine if you like sailing. I happen to get seasick."

Kate laughed. "I think I miss you already."

Ellie propped up her head with her right arm. "Don't say that."

Kate stared into Ellie's disconcerting blue eyes. "It's true. I haven't seen you for twenty-four years, and now I miss you. There's something about you."

Ellie's hands found Kate's waist and pressed her closer. "What is it?"

Kate wished she knew how to protect herself from this attraction. "It's your breasts. It's the way your body feels. It's our history. It's this," Kate whispered, her right hand touching Ellie's hip.

"Damn it, Kate." Ellie's eyes filled with tears. "I don't want to leave you."

Kate studied Ellie's high cheekbones, her long, straight forehead, her thin lips, her breasts rising and falling next to her. Without meaning to, without wanting to Kate allowed her hands to stroke Ellie's hair, let her body express what she could not say. As their breasts, legs, and hips touched, Kate gave in, lifted herself on top of Ellie, and leaned down to kiss her.

"Hey, there!" They jumped up and turned toward the road, where two men riding quarter horses had halted.

"Hello, Edward," Ellie called. "Hello, Ken. Beautiful day, isn't it? This is my friend Kate Paine."

Kate brushed herself off. Her legs were trembling, her pants were wet, and every sinew of her body was wired tight. She stood silently as Ellie chatted nonchalantly with the men about their children.

"One of these days," Ellie said after the men left, "I'm going to get caught."

"I think you just did," Kate reddened. "Do you do this with everybody?"

Ellie started up the hill toward their horses. "Of course not," she laughed. "Edward owns the grocery store in Turkey Run, and his son Justin is in my son Johnny's class." She stopped. "Is it too much for you, Katie? This family stuff?"

This double life, Kate thought to herself as she climbed into the saddle. She hadn't been around anyone so closeted since college; now she remembered why. Maybe it was good the men had come. Their presence had forced Kate to maintain the distance she had been ready to give up.

At the house she packed her things and tossed her bag in the back of the Honda.

"We had a nice time, didn't we?" Ellie said as they stood in the driveway.

"Very nice." Kate felt formal and self-conscious. "Thanks for inviting me."

"I want you to love riding as much as I do. I'm going to pester you until you come back."

"You'll be in Maine," Kate said, bothered by the almost kiss interrupted by the grocery man.

A car drove past Ellie's driveway. Ellie stepped back. When it had passed she kicked a pebble with her cowboy boot. "I'm not leaving for the East till next Thursday."

Kate opened her car door.

"I want to see you again, Katie. Please."

"Call me," Kate said, the midday sun burning her face. She felt restless, ready to go home, to her studio, to the rhythm of her life and the solitude of her house. "Thank you," she said, then slammed her car door and drove north to Sausalito.

As she passed through the brown hills, saw the blue calm of the sky, felt the cool of San Francisco and the Golden Gate, a strange thought occurred to her. What if she weren't able to get back to her old life? What if there never had been a life before Ellie? What if the memories of Ellie and their brief, explosive connection had burned for so long in Kate's mind that she could not retreat to her studio? What if she were compelled to play out whatever this revival of her friendship with Ellie would bring? Kate shivered. But Ellie was leaving for a month. That would give Kate time to come to her senses, to escape the call of Ellie's siren song.

Chapter **6**

Kate dropped her bag and sank onto the pale beige sofa, staring out at the oak trees. The water below in the bay was a deep blue. She scanned her studio, her eyes landing on the new painting of Gina and herself in the jungle, flowers closing around them. She looked at Gina's face; she felt nothing. She must be very tired.

She closed her eyes. If she could wake herself up, she could paint for two hours before her shift at the spa. The phone rang as she pulled on her shorts and her KEEP ON TRUCKIN' T-shirt.

"Katie? I've been calling all morning. Where were you?" It was Stacey.

"In Turkey Run."

"You spent the night?"

Kate told Stacey about her evening and the ride that morning. "When she was pregnant with her first son, she fell in love with a woman. They were lovers for five years." Kate opened the front door; the sun was getting hot. "She's had hundreds of girlfriends, Stace."

"What about her husband?"

"He doesn't say a word."

"I guess the rich live by different rules."

"She feels guilty, like it screwed up her son Simon. She was falling in love with Margo, she says, when she should have been falling in love with her baby."

Stacey paused. "Did things...heat up between you?"

Kate closed her eyes, leaning back against the sofa. "We went for a walk in the moonlight. And we kissed. But nothing more."

"She wants to sleep with you. I told you so. Where was the husband?"

"In bed. This morning he went to work." Kate coiled the phone cord around her arm.

"It's just a matter of time, Katie."

Kate stared at the painting of Gina. It was beautiful, even haunting, but Gina's face did not fill Kate with yearning. "You think so?"

Stacey laughed. "She puts on an entire dinner party so she can see you, tells you she's a raving lesbian, holds your hand under the full moon. The woman is ready, Kate."

The bougainvillea in the Gina painting needed a little more work. "Am I ready?"

"Sure you are."

"She's complicated, Stace."

"You don't have to marry the woman. Just have fun."

"I'm not good at fun."

Stacey laughed. "Don't be silly. What does the husband do?"

"He owns a crystal mine in Arkansas. My friend Claire says he gets involved in these bizarre business schemes and never makes any money."

"Doesn't have to if he has a trust fund."

"Claire says he's spent it."

"Does he know you and Ellie were involved as kids?"

"If what she says is true, they don't discuss anything." Kate hesitated. "If she calls, do you really think I should see her again?"

"Why not? She's safe. You can't get too involved. You can use her to practice having fun. Go slowly. Enjoy. It's a dream come true in a way. You'll get a chance to have what you were denied at school."

"Shouldn't I stop now, before anything gets started?"

Stacey laughed. "It's already started."

Ellie phoned the next day. "I loved the book." Kate had sent her Hemingway's novel *The Garden of Eden,* about a ménage, two women and a man, on the French Riviera. "Can I come tomorrow and spend the day?"

Kate thought of the work she had to do and her shift at the spa. She looked up at the wall, at Gina's face, which frowned, then faded from sight. "Sure," she said. "Come."

Chapter 7

Two white gardenias were Ellie's offering as she stood in the doorway, posture erect, gold-streaked hair shining, the smile on her face so radiant, it warmed Kate's studio in an instant.

"You made it." Kate bumped into the couch as she took the flowers and kissed Ellie's cheek. Her friend was already devouring the studio — the Gina jungle painting on Kate's easel, the mantle full of special shells from the beach, a photograph of Stacey and her cat, the tiny statue of Quan Yin, goddess of love and compassion, next to the orange votive candle. In the alcove by the bedroom, Ellie studied Kate's photographs of her friends and family, then stood at the window overlooking the bay, gazing down at the water.

"I love it here," Ellie said wistfully. "This is absolutely spectacular. The quintessential artist's cottage."

Kate wondered as she inhaled the sweet air now filled with the smell of Ellie's perfume if Ellie knew from her expression that Kate had thought about her every moment since she'd left Turkey Run on Friday. She stood next to Ellie, looking down at the bay and the Strawberry Peninsula across the water. "I got rid of my studio on Bridgeway when I stopped freelancing. I wish I had more room, but..." She felt as high as if she'd just smoked a joint of Claire's sinsemella. Did Ellie feel as breathless as she did?

"What would you like to drink?" In the old days Kate would have slugged a quick brandy to take the edge off. "I've got wine, beer, bourbon."

Ellie seemed surprised. "I've just had breakfast."

"Right." Kate sneaked a look at Ellie's eyes to find signs of obsession.

Ellie smiled. "I loved the book you sent me. I crawled into bed and read all weekend." Her blue eyes caught Kate's, then darted around the room.

"It reminded me of your life with Nicky and Margo in New York."

"Hemingway is such a chauvinist."

Kate blushed. She didn't know why; perhaps the novel wasn't the perfect gift after all. "Want coffee?"

"Had two cups already." Ellie twisted her fingers through her hair and looked at the painting of Gina. "I'm so awed by your work, Katie. By your being an artist."

"My father thinks I should get a job as a medical secretary."

Ellie stretched one arm along the back of the couch. "Isn't he a writer?"

Kate nodded. "He worries about me becoming homeless."

"But you've published a book, you've been in newspapers, you're having a show in October."

"I'm always on the edge financially." Kate reddened. When she was this uptight, she started inadvertently confessing things. She hadn't meant to. Nice girls from Miss Downey's never discussed money.

"You're very talented." Ellie tapped her fingers against the arm of the couch. The new painting of Kate and Gina seemed to interest her. "Is that Gina?"

Kate nodded.

As Ellie walked over to the painting, she released a new cloud of perfume. "What a beautiful woman." She leaned close, then stepped back.

Seeing Ellie had been easier in Turkey Run, at Ellie's house, where there was room to move. Here, in the small studio, the tension was unbearable.

"Want to go for a walk? I'm a little...nervous." There. She'd told the truth again. Said more than she'd needed to.

"Excellent idea." Ellie bolted out the door. "I'm a little nervous myself." She smiled and gave Kate a wink that ran from Kate's heart to her toes.

Better now, Kate thought as they walked down the driveway to the road, passing the large brown-shingled houses behind hedges of jasmine and pittosporum. She felt high and excited knowing that the lover of her childhood was inches from her, close enough to touch at any time.

"Sweet church." Ellie pointed to the brown shingled church with black trim and a gabled roof.

Kate nodded. "I went there for a while after my mother died. Thought I might be able to communicate with her. But she seems to prefer the ocean. See the cottage with bougainvillea? That's the rectory. The minister handcuffs his wife to the bed."

"You're funny." Ellie touched Kate's arm. "Did he mention that in a sermon?"

Kate shook her head. "My friend Stacey knows his wife from a hospice they volunteer for. The only way he can...do it is to torture her a little."

"That's good to know in case you ever need to blackmail him."

"Absolutely." Kate was laughing.

"So you were Episcopalian? Where'd you go to church?"

"Saint John's on Lafayette Square," Kate said.

"We went to Saint James's. In McLean."

Kate couldn't remember when she'd last been asked where she'd gone to church and which Protestant denomination she'd been raised in. Her friends in California meditated, chanted, went to the gay synagogue, held rituals under the full moon, but no one ever mentioned Episcopalians.

"I've never lost a parent," Ellie said, taking Kate's arm as they descended the steep staircase leading toward Bridgeway and the water. "Although I sometimes wish my mother were dead. She thinks I've gone to Sodom and Gomorrah."

"That must hurt."

"Maybe she's right," Ellie said, glancing sideways at Kate, then away.

The day was warm, and tourists swarmed the sidewalk taking pictures and pushing strollers. Kate and Ellie crossed the street by the low seawall.

The skyline of San Francisco was dreamlike across the water, even bluer where white sails leaned against it. In the distance was Angel Island, and off to the right, Alcatraz. Behind them, above Bridgeway, large houses clung to the cliffs.

"This is wonderful, Kate. How lucky you are."

Kate did feel lucky today. The air, the sun, the lapping waves slowed her racing heart. They took their time strolling along the water's edge. Ellie's arm had come to rest steadily against Kate's, making everything seem sexual — the sailboats shooting across the bay, the fishy smell of the water, the faded fabric of Ellie's orange jumpsuit as it touched Kate's forearm.

At the end of the seawalk, they sat down on a dock near the restaurant once owned by a famous San Francisco madam.

"Does your mother know about your relationships?" Kate asked, picking at some cerulean paint on her jeans that hadn't come out in the wash.

Ellie took off her sandals and dangled her feet over the water. Her feet were tan, wide, and strong, Kate saw. "We never talk directly. Margo came to Maine with us for years. Mother adored her, but she caught us in the pantry kissing one year, and she told Margo to get out. Said it was because of Margo's drinking."

"Nobody likes drunks," Kate said, tossing a pebble into the water.

Ellie waited for a man in blue jogging shorts and a Dallas Cowboys cap to pass. "Does your father know about you? He must."

Kate watched a yawl approach the cove from San Francisco Bay. "Actually my parents found out just after I'd graduated from Downey's. Because of Maria Eberts."

"Oh, my God. Maria Eberts." Ellie smiled. "What a babe!"

It was just so odd being here in California, 3,000 miles from Miss Downey's, talking with the girl she had fallen in love with at fourteen. Those years had been hard and lonely and painful. But here, where the past couldn't swallow Kate up, it was fun, exciting even, to talk with Ellie, now grown up, about their shared history.

"So what happened? With Maria Eberts?"

The yawl had lowered its sails, anchoring at a guest buoy in the cove. "We never really did anything. But I was crazy about her. After graduation she was supposed to come down and stay for a week at our house in Georgetown. I had it all planned out, this whole elaborate scenario of how I would tell her I was in love with her, and we'd get it on in my bedroom and live happily ever after. But she called to say she was in love with some boy from Harvard and wasn't coming."

"How mean!" Ellie said, moving closer.

Kate took a breath. "So my folks came home one night from a party and found me playing in my room with one of Alex's guns."

"Alex?"

"My father."

"Go on."

"I got morbidly attracted to this one particular gun."

Ellie's eyes widened.

"I loaded it and stuck the barrel in my mouth. And my parents walked in."

Ellie touched Kate's forearm. "Just because Maria Eberts loved a boy from Harvard? You were going to..."

Kate watched a group of tourists descend from a tour bus and walk toward the dock. She looked at Ellie. "I don't think I'd ever really recovered from what happened with you. It brought up all that old stuff that I'd never talked about with anyone. About you and all the love and the rejection. I finally told my parents the truth…"

"Did you tell them about me?"

Kate nodded. "And they freaked out and sent me to a mental hospital in Baltimore."

"Not Sheppard Pratt." Ellie's eyes widened.

"That's the one."

She squeezed Kate's knee. "That's where they send my aunt Grace when she has her depressions. Maybe you met her."

"Don't think so. But you'll appreciate this: My mother thought I should meet some nice boys before I took the cure. So they didn't lock me up until after my coming-out party."

Ellie sat up. "When you felt like killing yourself?"

"As long as I was drunk, the parties were bearable."

Ellie stared at Kate. "That's the way it is in Washington, isn't it? The daughter sticks a gun in her mouth, and the band plays on."

"Preferably Lester Lanin."

Ellie laughed and inched closer to Kate. "I'm sorry I hurt you, Katie. I didn't know what I was doing. You understand that, don't you?"

Kate nodded. "Neither did I."

"I want us to forget all that." She put an arm around Kate's shoulders. "I want to start over and — "

"Yo. Ladies!" A bearded man rowed a dinghy toward the dock. He waved, tossing his dock line to Ellie, who snagged it expertly to a cleat and offered him a hand up.

"Thanks a million, love," he grinned. "Would you ladies like to come aboard *Miranda*?" he said, pointing to the yawl.

Ellie looked at Kate.

"No thanks," Kate said.

"We'll pass."

He didn't move. "We've got a full bar. Anything you want to drink. She's a 52-foot Cape Cod — "

"My friend doesn't drink, and I've been aboard enough

boats to satisfy my curiosity for a lifetime." Ellie reached for Kate's hand and pulled her up.

"Suit yourself." The man walked away, scowling.

Kate was irritated that the man had interrupted their conversation. She felt better in the shadows of the redwoods and bay laurels as they walked back up the hill, out of the crowd and the sun.

In the cottage they unwrapped cracked crab and sourdough bread. The talk and walk had helped Kate relax, but now, so close to Ellie in such a small space, she felt painfully self-conscious. "Want some wine? Beer? Or there's brandy."

Ellie cracked a claw in her teeth. "For someone who doesn't drink, you seem to be very well-stocked."

Kate blushed. She had bought everything she thought Ellie might drink. But Ellie didn't seem to need it. Kate almost wished she did, wished Ellie'd get drunk and open up as she had last Thursday night. Instead they ate the crab in their fingers, sucking the white meat from the claws, dipping it in the bright-red hot sauce, rinsing it down with Calistoga, then pulling off hunks of sourdough bread. When they'd finished they washed their hands in the kitchen sink, and Kate made coffee, placing a mug in front of Ellie, who was staring down at the bay.

It's now or never, Kate thought. *This is not going to get any easier.* "Would you like to lie down?"

Ellie looked surprised. "Lie down?"

Kate blushed from head to toe. "I just thought — "

"I'd love to." Ellie jumped up. "I thought you'd never ask."

They lay like two girls at a slumber party, fully dressed under the green quilt. Heart pounding, Kate looked up at the sloping wooden ceiling above them, at the David Hockney poster of a vase of blue irises.

"It's wonderful here," Ellie said softly. Kate was afraid to move. Ellie's lips were inches from hers, her breath warm against Kate's cheek. The smell of her perfume and the proximity of her breasts made it hard to breathe. Was this bedazzling softness a fantasy?

"I've wanted to hold you ever since Hope and Raphael's," Ellie whispered.

"I wish you had," Kate said. "On Thursday night."

Ellie kissed Kate's neck, unbuttoning her red Hawaiian shirt. "I'm not her anymore, you know."

"Who?" Kate was aching.

"That proud Amazon you thought I was at eighteen." She smiled. "The one you had a crush on."

"Aren't you?" Kate raised her head to meet Ellie's lips. *Practice having fun,* Stacey had said. *You don't have to fall in love.* As they kissed, Ellie's lips, then her tongue reached into Kate's mouth. Kate fell into weightless space. Ellie was pulling Kate's shirt over her shoulders, her knee creating a delicious pressure on Kate's womb. Ellie's body was softer, more voluptuous than Gina's, which had been pounded into muscular perfection by aerobics and Nautilus. Kate slid below the quilt, wondering if this were really happening to her — Ellie Sereno, her childhood sweetheart, writhing on top of her, begging Kate for sex.

The wind chimes on the deck tinkled. Kate sat up.

"What's wrong?"

Kate rolled to her side. "You still have your clothes on." Heart skipping wildly, Kate unbuttoned Ellie's jumpsuit. When she saw the black lace bra, her breath caught. *Gina Lollobrigida. Sophia Loren.* She unfastened the snaps, amazed by the beautiful smooth breasts. "Do you mind?"

"Mind what?"

"If I kiss your breasts?"

"Jesus, no." Ellie pulled Kate down on her. Kate brushed her cheek back and forth, feeling the sea of soft skin, the hardening nipples, Ellie's hands cupping her butt.

"Suck me," Ellie whispered.

Yes. Her lips closed around a hardened nipple. Ellie was sweet, like vanilla and papaya. The taste, the hot fullness in her

mouth, the feel of Ellie's warm nipple on her tongue were turning Kate's womb to molten lava. She was Pat Boone making
love to Ann-Margret in *State Fair.* She was Cary Grant alone at
last with Doris Day. She was Marcello Mastroianni sliding
inside Anita Ekberg. Ellie lifted so Kate could peel off the bottom of the jumpsuit and toss it on the chair.

"It'll never be like this again," Ellie moaned, her fingers
pulling on Kate's hair.

"How do you mean?" Kate had found Ellie's clit, was slip-
ping quickly across its hard, silky surface.

"Shit." Ellie closed her eyes and let Kate climb inside her.
"Once we do this, everything will change."

"Will it?" Ellie was so fucking hot and wet.

"There won't be this need. This absolute necessity. This
wondering what you're feeling and thinking, this wondering if
you want to touch me as much as I want to touch you."

"I do," Kate whispered, her tongue licking Ellie's other
nipple, her fingers stroking Ellie back and forth, back and
forth.

"Now I won't have to guess what it's like to feel you inside
me and your elegant body on top of me."

"You held me once before," Kate said in and out, in and out
of Ellie's womb. "It didn't seem to take away the need or the
wondering. For either of us."

"But we're not those girls, Katie."

"Thank God."

"We're middle-aged women who've lived lifetimes. And yet
this..." Ellie began to arch, wrap her legs around Kate's waist
so that Kate could fit her entire hand inside her. "Feel so fucking good," she moaned. "Fuck!" she screamed, gripping Kate
like a trembling child. And then she cried.

Kate touched her gently, pressed the muscles of her back,
her fingers kneading, reading the powerful sinews, finding the
tightness in her cervical spine, sensing the explosive energy in
the lumbar spine behind her womb.

"I don't deserve this," Ellie cried.

"You do," Kate smiled, singing lightly as she rocked Ellie in her arms. "Remember that song 'Dream Lover' from when we were kids? About how every night Bobby Darin hopes and prays that this beautiful woman will be his?"

Ellie opened her eyes. "I'm not a dream. I'm real."

"I know," Kate smiled, humming what she remembered of the tune. "But you're magic to me."

"You really like me?"

Kate pulled back so she could gaze at the curved lips, the tanned now-pink cheeks, the blue eyes. "I can't get over the feel of you."

"Does it feel the same?" Ellie asked uncertainly.

"Better."

"And you like me?" Ellie traced Kate's nose and cheek and shoulder with her index finger.

"You were a rat for leaving me, but I still like you." Kate kissed Ellie's hair and neck and the soft place above her clavicle. "A lot."

"I'm not leaving you this time." Ellie rolled onto her back and pulled Kate on top of her. "I want you to fuck me again. I've waited twenty-four years."

Kate laughed. She laughed, and she reached into Ellie's body with her lips and her tongue and her mouth and her fingers and her heart, kissing all of Ellie's silky places, kneading the tight ones, listening with her hands to the whispers and contours and contractions of Ellie's skin and pulse and nerves. She was fucking Ellie, loosening her, opening her, going places where silence and fear and secrecy were stored like sharp knives ready to kill. "Yes," Ellie cried, coming and crying and coming again. "Please, Kate."

The smell of suntan oil and salt and summer rose from their skin as Kate heard the tune playing somewhere in her mind on that little yellow radio she had as a girl. It was about a woman, about loving that woman so much, wanting her for so long that the dream of her becomes more real than the woman herself.

□ Part II □

Chapter **8**

The sky was a gray glare over Long Island Sound, the air
humid and heavy. Ellie stretched out on her towel and
squinted down at shallow water. Nathan was dancing in the
sand next to the baby-sitter near the waves, clapping happily
as the bigger children played in the surf. From this distance
Nathan seemed almost normal, a long way from the day in his
future when baby-sitters couldn't handle him, when he would
be six foot three like his brothers but wearing diapers and
unable to speak or tie his shoes. How ironic that her sweetest
child, the one she loved best, would never achieve anything.

Across the sound she could see the low green of the
Connecticut shore. In the cove Johnny and Simon were windsurfing with their cousin Alphie, striped sails whizzing out into
deeper water. Ellie had chosen this spot so she could be alone,
away from the swimming pool and the Piping Rock clubhouse,
where, on the patio, beneath blue and white parasols, mothers
and grandmothers in cotton print dresses and canvas deck
shoes were entertaining their children and grandchildren. Ellie
was not yet ready to face the van Meters, the Whitneys, the
Underwoods; she felt fat and exposed in her bathing suit,
needed time to collect herself, time away from Nicky's father
and stepmother, Helen, time to read Kate's letter.

Mr. Webster had handed her the manila envelope after breakfast this morning. "For you," he'd said, raising an eyebrow. Kate had followed directions, leaving no return address. All morning Ellie had tried to take an interest in Nicky and his parents' talk of their friends — illnesses, divorces, grandchildren, and cousins who'd been booted from prep school, accepted by Yale, graduated from law school. But what she longed for was a moment alone to read Kate's letter.

She turned over on her stomach, checked again on Nathan and the boys, then slit open the envelope with her finger. *Thank you, Katie.* It was a ten-page handwritten letter. Kate had enclosed three large black-and-white photographs. In the first Ellie was helping Dotty's son onto Monkey, face concentrated, hand shortening a stirrup. The next was Sausalito, the first night Ellie had stayed over, lying on Kate's couch, knees up, cozy under the quilt, fire blazing in the fireplace. Ellie was surprised and amazed by her expression; she looked blissful, her eyes soft, her mouth relaxed in a half smile. In the third photograph, taken by Jamie after the Ping-Pong match, Kate and Ellie were side by side, arms around each other, smiling. Ellie was slightly drunk, giddy even, and Kate looked sleek and aristocratic, like a racehorse, despite the spiked blond hair and jersey shirt and jeans. Ellie kissed the photograph, could almost feel Kate's arms around her as she read the letter.

The sun flared out from behind a cloud, and suddenly the sound was royal blue instead of gray. With damp sandy fingers Ellie groped through her straw beach bag and found a stubby golf pencil she had taken from Mr. Webster's desk this morning. She would write Kate, tell her —

"Mom?" Simon stood over her, face taut, dripping and breathless in his blue-jean cutoffs. "I can't find Johnny."

Ellie stared at her tall, handsome, oldest son. "What?"

Simon's hair was wet, his body shivering. "He turned over way, way out there in the sound."

Ellie leaped up, eyes searching the water. Nathan was still playing with the baby-sitter, and there were no sails in the cove.

"God help him," Ellie whispered as she saw the crowd gathering by the lifeguard's wooden throne.

"I thought he was right next to me," Simon was saying as they ran to the small outboard skiff the lifeguard was pushing into the water.

"I'm his mother," Ellie said.

"Come on." He gave her a hand, and Simon followed. They buzzed across the sound as the lifeguard talked over a walkie-talkie, scanning the water for Johnny's sail.

"Why the hell did you go out so far?"

Simon's face was ashen as he strained over the waves looking for his brother. "I thought everything was okay. But he couldn't get back in."

Please, let him be okay. Don't let anything happen. Not to Johnny.

The lifeguard leaned forward. "He can swim, can't he?"

"Of course," Simon yelled.

"Was he wearing a life preserver?"

Ellie glanced at Simon, who shook his head.

Shit! She searched the waves, choppier now, as the breeze picked up. *I'll do anything. I'll be a good wife. I'll give up Kate.* Her gut was a black pit as they bounced across the sound, began to approach the Connecticut shore. Thunderheads were forming in front of them. The lifeguard had called the U.S. Coast Guard; a rescue boat was on its way from Oyster Bay.

"There he is!" Simon screamed. "I see his sail." A blue-and-yellow-striped sail bobbed in the water; there was no sign of Johnny.

Then Ellie saw him, facedown in the water.

"Johnny?"

His body seemed inert as Simon and the lifeguard hauled him into the skiff. As soon as he was inside, he began coughing. He coughed, and then he threw up, and Ellie wrapped him in a towel.

"You're going to be okay, Johnny." She held him in her arms as they lurched through the surf toward the beach. "What happened?"

"Got too tired," he whispered. "Couldn't get righted."

A crowd was waiting on the beach as they climbed from the skiff. "You're not windsurfing anymore, either of you," Ellie said, helping Johnny up the beach, arms around his shoulders.

"Next time we won't go out so — "

"There won't be a next time, Si," Ellie snapped, beckoning Nathan and the baby-sitter. Louise van Meter waved to Ellie from the deck of the beach club as Ellie buckled Nathan's seat belt and hurried the boys into the car. Johnny seemed to have his color back, but he couldn't stop shivering.

"What's the hurry, Mom?"

Ellie waved to Louise van Meter. "I've got a hungry child and a drowned boy. Have to get home."

"Will we see you at tomorrow's party?" called the handsome white-haired woman, who wore a navy skirt and white cotton blouse.

"Absolutely." Ellie glanced at Johnny. "How do you feel, my sweetheart? Should I take you to the hospital?"

"No way." He ate one of Nathan's cookies. "Feel great."

In moments they were crossing the marsh in the Websters' weathered Jeep. Ellie studied the Baldings' huge gray-shingled beach house, where she had gone to many parties as a teenager and played spin the bottle with Billy Balding.

"You can't see much of the ruling class on the North Shore," she had told Kate. "They're hidden behind long driveways and high fences. But you can feel them, feel your shortcomings reflected in their manicured lawns, their perfect, suntanned bodies, their starchy white tennis dresses."

On the right, as they passed the shaded entrance to the Creek Club, Ellie thought of her grandmother, who had always arranged each summer for Ellie to escape the claustrophobic, humid summers of northern Virginia. She'd loved her grandmother's quiet white farmhouse on the Jericho Turnpike, which was impossibly noisy now, bumper-to-bumper traffic on weekends. The house had been turned into a popular bar and grill, and Nina was dead.

Ellie had never really felt secure visiting Long Island: Most of the children considered Virginia as remote as Tierra del Fuego; they expected Ellie to wear her hair in cornrows and go barefoot. You didn't belong here unless you went to the Greenvale School, then off to Westover or Farmington or Concord. Thank God for Catherine, Nicky's younger sister, who hadn't cared that Ellie was not from Long Island, who shared her ponies and swimming pool and the creek down the hill from the Websters' house, where they caught crayfish in tin cans and played for hours.

"Mom, let's stop for Slurpees," Simon yelled as they approached Locust Valley, a village consisting of a few low buildings straddling the tracks of the Long Island Railroad.

"No way. Johnny almost drowned."

They passed the Piping Rock Golf Club, then turned onto Chicken Valley Road with its maples and beeches and dogwoods and few remaining elms.

"Mom!" Johnny yelled. Ellie had almost missed the Websters' driveway, obscured by the leaning dogwood trees, which in the spring were pink and white and unbelievably lovely. The sight of the Websters' three-story Georgian brick house, settled smugly on the crest of the hill, shaded by elms and a spreading beech, filled Ellie with pride and dismay.

"Mrs. Webster thought you must have eaten at the beach club," Hannah, the cook, told her. "We went ahead with lunch."

"We're starved." Ellie grabbed a beer and a sandwich from the fridge, retreating to her room upstairs at the far end of the hall. Closing the heavy green window curtains, she switched on the air conditioner and pushed back the satin folds of the pale green eiderdown. Reaching for Kate's letter, holding it next to her heart, she felt a shiver of comfort. Only four days on Long Island and Ellie was ready to go home; Johnny had almost drowned, and the thought of one more week in the bosom of Nicky's family exhausted her.

She had to pull herself together. She needed some clarity before seeing Nicky and the Websters. They would think her a bad mother for Johnny's near drowning.

Kate loves me, she thought, buoyed by the tender feelings in her breast. Taking out the picture of herself with Kate the night of the dinner party, she stared into Kate's eyes. There was something about their clarity, their independence, their wisdom that Ellie found enormously comforting. Was it that Kate had never expected a man to take care of her, never told lies? Some lesbians frightened Ellie with their separatism and anger and mannishness, but Kate, whom Ellie had known as an awkward and admiring fourteen-year-old, felt very safe.

She picked up the phone and dialed. "Sweetheart," she said softly, "it's Ellie."

"Is it really you?" Kate's voice was happy, surprised.

"Thank you for your letter, my darling. I love the photographs." The wire hissed and crackled.

"I can't stop thinking about you."

"Keep thinking about me, Katie. I need that. Johnny almost drowned today, and I'm ready to come home."

"What happened?"

"He capsized." Ellie heard footsteps. They had so little time. "You are the only thing keeping me alive here, in the bosom of Nicky's family."

"I can't hear you very well."

"I'm under constant surveillance." She looked at Nicky's linen suit hanging in the closet. "Do you really love me? You said in your letter — "

"I'm crazy about you." Kate's voice faded in and out.

"Why? Tell me why. I feel so shitty."

"Because when I was fourteen years old and you were seventeen, you had the most beautiful breasts I'd ever seen."

Ellie's throat tightened. Always her breasts. "I'm not that person anymore, Kate. I'm soft and flabby."

"Remember Yeats?" Kate had sent her a poem that had stopped Ellie's heart. " 'It had become a glimmering girl, with apple blossoms in her hair, who called me by my name and ran and faded in the brightening air.' "

"Katie…" She heard a car pulling into the driveway.

"I'm the wandering Aengus in the Yeats poem, chasing the glimmering girl."

"I've got to go."

"Hello?" A male voice had picked up the phone.

"Mr. Webster? It's Ellie. I'm just getting off." The receiver clicked. Sweat dampened Ellie's forehead. "I'll call you tomorrow. Keep writing." She slammed down the receiver.

Lying on the bed, she pulled up the quilt and closed her eyes, moving her hand slowly against herself, thinking of Kate's arms, forgetting the pact she had made with God on the Long Island Sound.

Chapter **9**

When Nicky came to bed, Ellie pretended to be asleep.
"Lili?" He edged closer.

"Please, Nicky."

"It's been so long," he whispered, lifting her nightgown.

"In the morning, Nickers."

"Why not now?"

Ellie didn't answer.

"I'm your husband, Lili."

The words stabbed Ellie with guilt. She rolled onto her back, imagined Kate's arms, her smooth skin, her loving touch as Nicky moved inside her. She was glad he couldn't see her tears when he whispered "Thank you" and fell asleep.

In the dark Ellie fumbled for her robe, tiptoeing down the wide wooden staircase into the kitchen, with its comforting smell of vanilla and bread. Turning on the light, she sat down at the kitchen table. When she spied Hannah's grocery pad resting on the familiar flowered oilcloth, she picked up a pencil and wrote "Kate" at the top. Just writing her name was a comfort. "Dream Lover, where are you?" she began. "I'm in the kitchen. Nicky and I have just made love." She stopped, crying too hard to write.

In Mr. Webster's book-lined den, she inhaled the smell of leather and Balkan Sobranie pipe tobacco and poured herself a glass of brandy, staring at the photograph taken last summer of the Websters with Nicky and the boys. There was Simon, making a face at the camera; Johnny, smiling as always; Nathan, climbing onto Ellie's lap. They passed for a happy family.

Nina had approved of that family, hadn't she? Ellie's grandmother had been responsible for Ellie's marriage to Nicky seventeen years ago, although she would have bitterly denied it. Ellie's grandfather, an outstanding polo player and mediocre insurance broker, knew everyone on the North Shore. And so did Nina. She made sure Ellie met all the right people when she came up with her family on visits from Virginia. The summer Ellie was sixteen and dating two boys from Locust Valley, Nina told her she was too undisciplined for her own good. She didn't approve of the way Ellie chased, then dropped the boys who pursued her — something she'd been doing ever since her sinewy body had erupted into a full-breasted woman's at thirteen.

"I'm paying for your education, Ellie, not your recreation," her grandmother had said of Ellie's long college weekends skiing at Sugarbush and Mount Snow. "We have to marry you early and well."

After college Ellie found a job teaching music at a private girls school in Manhattan. But she had hated rising early each morning, eating lunch in the teachers' room, working until 4 o'clock day after day. She dreamed of traveling, of skiing in Europe, of jet-setting with the beautiful people. After two years she quit her job.

"It's as easy to fall in love with a rich man as a poor one," Nina had told her.

"But Dad wasn't rich," Ellie argued.

"And that's fine," her grandmother said. "But with your style and good looks, you can have anyone you chose."

Ellie poured another brandy. No one had ever expected her to do anything useful with her life. Her mother thought she was hedonistic and unfocused; her grandmother decided that a year abroad would mature her, round out her education, give her a chance to use her French.

Six months later, in Innsbruck, Ellie met Andrew Mathews, a world-class skier from Boston. Ellie loved his masculine confidence, his humor, his angular good looks. But she played with him, had slept with that silly ski instructor with the amazing blue eyes to make him jealous. When Andrew broke it off, she returned to New York, hurt and confused. She had never been rejected by a man. She was twenty-five years old, and most of her friends were married.

She had picked up the phone and called Nicky Webster, who had adored her since their grandmothers had introduced them as children. Nicky proposed to her at '21,' and Ellie accepted.

"Marry Nicky Webster?" her grandmother said when Ellie told her over tea in the den of her house on Jericho Pike. "I don't think that's a good idea."

Ellie was stunned. "But you introduced us. And Nicky adores me."

"I'm sure he adores you. Many men adore you."

"Mrs. Webster was one of your closest friends."

"My closest friend. And his stepmother is a saint. But you mustn't marry Nicky."

"What's wrong with him?" Ellie had thought Nicky was everything her grandmother valued.

"He's a very odd young man."

"He's not a fairy," Ellie said quickly.

"Why on earth would you say such a thing? Of course, he's not. But his mother's death knocked something out of him, my darling."

Nina had been playing bridge at Piping the year the club manager appeared at her table and announced in a whisper that the Wilkes-Hensons' au pair had been rowing the children in a dinghy in Cold Spring Harbor when she'd stumbled across a woman's body in the cockpit of *Desire,* the

Websters' sloop. It was Victoria Webster, Nicky's mother. She'd been shot in the head. Some said it was murder, but most, including the Oyster Bay police, thought it was suicide.

"I'll never forgive Will Webster for sending Nicky away to Saint Paul's so soon after. Will Webster is a very shrewd businessman, but he's a cold human being," her grandmother said. "Catherine's the only one of the Webster children with any moxie."

"His mother died a long time ago, Nina." Ellie fought tears. "Nicky's fine now."

Nina poured another cup of tea. "You're not in love with him, Ellie. You would have married him years ago if you were."

What Nina didn't understand was that not loving Nicky made it easier to marry him. She had learned from Andrew that being too in love can hurt. And Ellie liked Nicky's self-absorption; it gave her freedom. She didn't want a man who paid close attention to her. Sometimes he seemed to forget she was even in the room with him.

"At least wait another year," her grandmother pleaded. But Ellie had made up her mind.

Beaming, Nicky came down to breakfast, kissing Ellie's cheek. Her head ached, and her throat was dry. "I loved last night," he whispered.

Ellie stiffened. Simon, who had spilled some sugar on the mahogany table, was shaping it into neat lines with his knife. Was he pretending to chop cocaine? "Simon, stop it!" she said, more caustically than she'd intended.

Nicky touched her arm. "It's early, Lili. Let him be."

Ellie's eyes narrowed. "I don't want him taking drugs."

"Jesus, Mom! I'm arranging rows of sugar."

Ellie's hands shook as she poured herself coffee. "You're hurting the table, and you're doing something that looks very much like chopping lines of cocaine."

"How would you know?" Simon taunted her.

That moment she hated her son, so pale and handsome and insolent. "You have enough problems as it is without taking drugs."

"Thanks, Mom. I love you too." Simon pushed away from the table. "What time are we leaving for the city, Dad?"

"Long Island Railroad," Nicky said, already absorbed in his *Wall Street Journal*. Nathan laughed wildly, banging his plastic cup on the high chair.

Ellie glanced at Nicky. "Isn't tonight Simms's party at Piping? Can you get to the city and back by five?"

"Count me out of the party," Simon said, tossing a tennis ball across the floor for the Websters' corgi.

Ellie took the sticky cup from Nathan's sticky hand. "Simms Newcomb was a dear friend of your great-grandmother's."

"Your mother wants you to go and pay homage. Simms Newcomb was your great-grandmother's entrée into North Shore society," Nicky said, his eyes still fixed on the paper.

Ellie put down her coffee. "My grandmother had all the friends she could possibly want on the North Shore."

"Her boyfriend couldn't take her *everywhere*. He had a wife, after all." Nicky was reading the stock market quotes.

"Great-grandmother had a boyfriend?" Delighted, Simon came back to the table.

Ellie's head was pounding. "My grandmother was thirty years old when her husband died. She had no money and two little girls. Her friend, Mr. Jennings, was married, but not happily, to a woman he did not live with."

"How come?" Simon tossed the ball again for Sam, the corgi.

"His wife lived in a mental hospital," Nicky said. "She was a schizophrenic."

"Really?"

"Foster Jennings was a Roman Catholic, and in those days Catholics couldn't divorce."

Nicky had finally stopped reading the paper. "Foster Jennings wouldn't have married your great-grandmother even if the church had allowed him. Your great-grandmother was a Jew."

"Nicky!"

Johnny's eyes widened. "How come you never told us, Mom?"

Ellie wasn't ready for this, not before breakfast. "Nina was an Episcopalian."

"Your great-grandmother was a Jew and a card player, Simon." Nicky was enjoying himself immensely. "Her father shoed horses in Virginia, near Warrenton. Her specialty was bridge, but she won at any card game she tried — poker, blackjack, canasta. She amassed a small fortune beating some of the North Shore's finest families."

Johnny and Simon stared at their mother; Nathan giggled, throwing orange slices from his high chair.

"Was she, like, a criminal?" Simon grinned.

"Of course not." Ellie hated smug Nicky's implication that her bloodlines were somehow tainted, genetically inferior to his. "Nina's husband was from an old New York family, but he had no money when he died. Nina had never been to college, had no career, no way to earn a living, so she gambled. She was very smart and beautiful and fun, and people loved losing to her. They had plenty of money, and they knew she could use it. She put all of her grandchildren through college on her winnings, including me."

"I wish I'd known her," Simon said. "She sounds cool."

"She was. I'm sorry you never had the chance." Ellie wiped her eyes.

Nicky said, "Your great-grandmother cared about one thing — for her children and grandchildren to marry well. That's why she brought Ellie here each summer."

"It worked too." Simon spun the lazy Susan in the middle of the table. "You used to be rich, didn't you, Dad, before you spent it all?"

Nicky was no longer amused, but Simon wouldn't let up. "Did you marry Dad for his money, Mom? Like your grandmother wanted?"

"Drop it, Simon," Johnny said quietly.

"It had nothing to do with money. Your father and I met as children and ran into each other when he was at Saint Paul's." Nicky was eyeing her curiously. "We passed in the clock tower. He was going up, and I was going down, and our eyes met on the staircase, and something happened."

"Just passing in the clock tower?" Simon's brown eyes studied her. "I don't get it."

"Neither do I," Ellie said.

She could feel Nicky's eyes on hers as he wiped his mouth with his napkin. "At one time in our lives," he said slowly, "your mother and I were very much in love."

Ellie unloosened Nathan's bib. "Your father fell in love with my breasts," she said tightly, "and I fell in love with his back."

The boys laughed nervously.

Ellie's eyes fixed on the small ivory-handled fruit knife on the breakfast table. How easy it would be to grab it now. Nicky would be dead in seconds if she aimed for the kidneys or — better yet — turned and plunged it into his heart.

She walked out of the room, her hands in fists by her sides.

Chapter **10**

Thrusting the letter she'd written into her handbag, Ellie sank into her sister-in-law's green Mercedes, which smelled of perfume and leather and Catherine's charmed life. Nicky and the boys had left for the city on the Long Island Railroad — he was meeting with his trust officer — and the boys were excited by the prospect of roaming New York with their father.

Catherine was unchanged: handsome and kind, her graying hair untouched, cheeks pink, her blue eyes clear — a more forgiving, less imperious version of Nicky. Slender as always, she never let herself get out of control like Ellie, eating to fill the hole inside her. Catherine didn't have a hole inside her.

"How are you, Lili?" she asked, giving Ellie a kiss. "Tell me about you and the boys."

In this comfortable car on this clear August day, the North Shore looked green and idyllic, not nearly as terrible as it had an hour earlier. "Everything's great," Ellie began, bursting into tears.

Catherine slowed and put an arm around Ellie's shoulder. "What's wrong?"

Damn. She had to keep these emotions under control. *Nothing is really wrong.* In a few minutes she and Catherine would be weaving through the green lush trails of the North Shore on horseback. "You know what these visits are like." The tears kept coming. She took the Kleenex Catherine held out to her. "So many expectations. And memories."

Catherine stroked Ellie's hair. "Are things better with Nicky?"

Was she so obvious? Of course, Catherine had been there last summer when Nicky had exploded at Ellie at Sunday dinner in front of all the family. Ellie couldn't remember what the argument had been about, but the Bloody Marys had fueled the fire. If only she could tell Catherine about Kate, about her fear that her marriage was about to become unraveled. But how could she? No matter how sympathetic Catherine was, her loyalty had to be to her brother, to propriety, to maintaining the status quo.

"Nothing's really changed." Ellie blew her nose. "Half the time Nicky's trying to sell his crystal mine, the other half he talks about buying another one. I'm afraid the whole thing is going to go belly-up, and he keeps trying to get our friends to invest. It's embarrassing."

"Poor Nicky." Catherine turned at the light. "He should have been a teacher or a lawyer. Anything but a businessman."

"I'm afraid I'm not much help. I'm terrible at math. You know that. But I have a feeling about this crystal thing, and it isn't good." Ellie spied a mailbox farther on. "Can we stop for a second?" Taking the letter from her handbag, she leaped from the car.

"Must be someone special."

"The mortgage." Lying was something Ellie had been doing for so long, it came automatically, even when unnecessary.

"How are you really, Ellie?" Before she started the car, Catherine turned in her seat. "How's Margo?"

Ellie blushed. She had never told Catherine the nature of her relationship with Margo, but Catherine had heard too many stories not to know something. "She lives in Santa Fe now, with Emma, raising iguanas."

Catherine laughed.

"Something like that. She's quit drinking. Their lives are very...peaceful." She stopped herself. Why did it make her so sad and uncomfortable to say that? Was it envy?

"Everything okay with the boys?" Catherine went on quickly.

Ellie blew her nose. "Some days I think Simon's actually getting a little nicer, and then he'll do something like call me a bitch or come home stoned. I can't seem to do anything with him. But Johnny's a dream."

"And Nathan?" Catherine asked softly.

Ellie stared out at a rolling pasture. "Helen has found a divine baby-sitter. Both the boys are in love with her."

As they approached the white fences, shingled barns, and neat paddocks at the stables, Ellie started to feel human again. Kate would hate the club's locked gates and crusty Republican members, but Ellie needed desperately to be on a horse. On a horse she could not possibly feel so beaten.

In the barn Catherine lifted a saddle and bridle from the trunk by her stall. "Will you ride Scandal?"

"I'd love to."

"She's been spooky. Megan won't ride her. I thought you might be able to do something with her. Are you game?"

When Ellie had ridden the Peruvian Paso last summer, she'd fallen in love with her fast, smooth gait. "Absolutely."

The smell of manure and oats and horses helped erase the memory of breakfast this morning. She brushed the sleek chestnut horse, feeling lighter as she followed the smooth contours of Scandal's powerful flanks. Her world might be falling apart, but today she was going to ride a brilliant horse on fabulous trails through the most exquisite horse country in America. Even in borrowed britches and tight boots, she felt free with a powerful mare moving beneath her.

Catherine called as they reached the long, sloping meadow where they always galloped. "Ready?" Ellie nodded. "Here we go."

If only Ellie could bottle this exhilaration. Catherine was just ahead, leaning forward, bottom up, just out of the saddle, hands close to her horse's neck. If only Kate were here. If only —

From the left something moved suddenly — a bird, a squirrel — and Scandal shied, bucking. Losing a stirrup, Ellie grabbed the horse's mane, dropping deep into her legs. Scandal was galloping out of control. They passed Catherine, tore up to the top of the hill, down the next. Ellie pulled so hard on the reins, her arms hurt. The horse slowed at last, cresting the hill. Ellie was trembling by the time Catherine caught up.

"You can see why Megan won't ride her."

"It was my fault. I was thinking about something else and lost my concentration." Ellie patted the mare's long, smooth neck. "We're fine, aren't we, Scandal?" She had not felt so happy since her last evening with Kate.

But what if Ellie had fallen? No one would have known to call the one person in the world she would want told. Shouldn't she tell Catherine about her life and Kate? "Catherine?"

She turned.

But Ellie could not move her lips. "I'm...I'm very happy riding with you."

Later, when Catherine dropped her at the Websters', she turned off the engine. "I know how brave you are, Ellie, but you don't have to do the stiff-upper-lip thing with me. You can tell the truth. We were friends long before — "

"Sweetheart." Ellie felt tears again. "You're the best."

"I mean it."

Ellie swallowed. "I'm such a failure."

"That's not true. You're a wonderful person who's been...dealt a complicated hand." They both wiped tears away. "I wish you weren't so far away. I wish you were right next door, and we could ride every day and not have to shrink our whole lives into a few hours once a year." Blowing her nose, Catherine inhaled, squaring her shoulders. "Aren't we two the silly ones? See you tonight? At Simms's birthday?"

Ellie waited for her to turn the car around, waving good-bye. She was crying when she dialed Kate in California. She needed to hear Kate's voice, to have some reassurance that Kate was still there and loving her. But the machine picked up.

Chapter **11**

"**A**re we late?" Ellie closed the rear door of the Websters' Mercedes, irritated because she hadn't been able to reach Kate. Nicky had returned from the city with a brand-new suit, without the boys, and with no concern as to how they'd find their way back.

"Nicky says the boys decided not to come," Mrs. Webster said.

"Can you believe it?" Ellie sighed.

"I don't know why you people can't control your children." Mr. Webster had already had a few cocktails.

"They're teenagers, Jimmy," said his wife. "I'm sure you were the same way at seventeen."

"I damned as hell wasn't. I did what I was told or the old man locked me in the icehouse."

Ellie looked at Nicky, who was gazing out the window, cheeks flushed. He must have had a drink while Ellie dressed.

"I did the same thing to Nicky when he was disrespectful."

"Didn't know we had an icehouse," Nicky said absently.

They turned into the Piping Rock drive, where, half a mile away, the pale gray clubhouse stood imposingly on the rise of green lawn above the fairway. The stables and carriage houses where Ellie's grandfather and great-uncle had kept their polo ponies now housed mowers, tractors, and ailing golf carts. Ellie counted seven Jaguars in the parking lot.

"Club looks great," Nicky said as they approached.

"It should," grumbled his father. "They raised our dues another fifteen hundred. Remodeled the whole damned place for the Jews. They want everything new."

"Piping has always had Jews, Jimmy," Mrs. Webster said calmly. "Mr. Otto Kahn was Jewish."

"Otto Kahn gave the damned land to start the club. They had to let him in."

Wincing, Ellie glanced around as the Websters went to greet their friends. She made her way to the ballroom, where a handsome man with snowy hair and an amused smile was greeting the guests.

"Happy Birthday, Mr. Newcomb," Ellie said. "It's Ellie."

"Of course." Simms Newcomb pumped her hand, kissing her cheek. "So glad you're here. Where's Nicky?" He turned to another old friend of her grandmother's, Stokes Cunningham. "Ellie's husband owns a crystal mine, Stokes. In Arkansas, isn't it, Ellie?" He patted Ellie's arm. "You believe those crystals have healing properties?"

"That's Nicky's department. I'll go find him. Let him give you the lowdown." She needed a drink.

Two blue eyes peered at her as she entered the bar.

"Ellie?" The man wore horn-rimmed glasses, a khaki suit, and yellow bow tie; blond hair tumbled over the collar of his jacket.

"Billy?" Billy Savage was one of the few Washington boys Ellie had really liked as a girl. Although half of his family were horse people from Charlottesville, his great-grandfather had been a U.S. congressman from New York and a liberal. Billy had ridden a Harley, worn a black leather jacket, and always carried his sixteen-millimeter movie camera with him. They'd met at a dance and senior year, over spring vacation, had planned a hiking trip along the Appalachian Trail. It would have been the weekend Ellie lost her virginity if only the skies hadn't opened and poured rain for three days straight. They'd canceled the trip and never had another date; Billy had gone on to Columbia and Ellie to Bennington. Sitting next to him now, she wondered how different her life might have been if the weather had been fair that weekend years ago.

Billy was a filmmaker in New York. Ellie had seen his documentary on the war in Nicaragua at a benefit in Palo Alto several years ago. Two days before it was to air, PBS had canceled the film under pressure from the president; the film proved that Ronald Reagan, had personal knowledge of the arms-for-hostages deal with the contras. Ellie had always admired the confidence with which Billy raised hell against the WASP elites who raised him.

"You look terrific." Billy gave her a warm hug. "Do you have a minute?"

Ellie could think of nothing she would rather do than talk with Billy Savage. He was leading her into the members library, a dark wood-paneled room with high ceilings, walls of trophies in glass cases, huge leather armchairs, and photographs of the club's early days.

"How's showbiz?"

"Have you heard about the new film?"

"If you're raising money, I'm afraid Nicky and I are — "

"Don't be silly." He leaned forward. "It's about the OSS. The CIA before it was the CIA." Billy moved closer. "Simms Newcomb has agreed to an interview."

"Simms?"

"He was CIA. Surely you knew."

"Simms started a business after the war."

"A spy business," Billy said softly. A man and a woman entered the library, saw them talking, and sat down in another corner.

Ellie sipped her gin and tonic. "Air Cargo International?" She noticed a small, oddly attractive scar on Billy's chin.

"Anti-Communists International," Billy smiled. "That was its nickname. Wherever there are Communists, Air Cargo is there, supplying guns, personnel, whatever is needed to get rid of them."

Did Billy know her father had worked for Air Cargo years ago?

"Your dad went to Yale, didn't he? Joined OSS in his sophomore year and went to Air Cargo after the war."

Ellie laughed. "You know more about my family than I do."

"Half our friends' parents in Washington were CIA, Ellie. Your father too."

"Come on, Billy."

Billy looked toward the door. "Spent a lot of time in Miami, didn't he — around the time of the Bay of Pigs?"

"Billy!" She had no idea what her father did during all his travels, only that she had hated his being away so much.

Billy loosened his tie. "While we were kids worrying about dancing class and getting into college, our fathers and half their friends were planning coups and covert actions all over the world. All the guys we thought were lawyers for the government were CIA. Did you know that in Indonesia, half a million Indonesians were killed in the CIA-backed coup?" Billy watched her face eagerly. "Air Cargo Express flew most of those weapons in. I wouldn't be surprised if your father had been in on that."

"That's ridiculous." What was ridiculous, she realized, was the fact that she had no idea what her father had done at ACI. Still, she was bothered by Billy's assertion that her father was a spy.

Billy sipped a bottle of Perrier. He'd stopped drinking after a motorcycle accident in Florida. He'd been shooting a documentary on the Everglades. "Spies and alcoholics, Ellie. That's our heritage."

"Dad wasn't even political. Why would he work for the CIA?"

"Thrills and chills? I don't know." Billy shrugged. "But I'd like to interview your father. Can you help me out?"

Ellie was startled. "Why would he tell you if he's never even talked about it to me?"

"Sometimes they like to get things off their chests." Billy took a business card from his wallet. "He's no longer with the agency — he may want to talk. They were powerful once. Deposed leaders, toppled governments. A lot of them thought of themselves as heroes. But what they did never makes it into history books. It's still going on. Talbot Coe out there" — Billy pointed at the doorway — "Nicky's buddy from the Yale crew team, is building shopping centers in Saudi Arabia. He works for the agency. Nippy Spense, ambassador to Honduras, is up to his ears." He brushed his hair off his face. "The CIA signed up tons of bright young Yalies: idealistic, smart — perfect for their purposes. So the next time you see your father — "

"I really don't — "

"I've put you on the spot." Billy touched her hand. "Sorry, Ellie. I forget that not everybody finds this as intriguing as I do." He pushed his glasses up on his nose. "Tell me how you are."

How could she make her life sound interesting to someone like Billy? "What do you want to know?"

Billy's blue eyes studied her. "How's Nicky?"

If she said a word about her marriage, she would burst into tears, as she had this morning with Catherine. She grabbed another cigarette from her purse. "These visits east take their toll."

"All the North Shore Brahmins on their last gasp," he nodded.

"They feel pretty powerful to me."

"The longer you put it off, Ellie, the more powerful they'll seem."

"Put what off?" Ellie bristled, brushing a thread from her black dress.

"I met a friend of yours last fall. Margo Whitby," he said, moving closer. "At a fund-raiser in New York for the OSS film. She was with Emma."

He knows, Ellie thought. *Margo told him.* For the rest of her life, Margo would make her pay for not leaving Nicky.

"Things aren't like they were when we were kids. It's not a sin to be a lesbian. My wife's brother is gay. We have lots of gay friends." He touched her arm.

Ellie pulled away. "That's enough, Billy." She rose and turned to the door. Billy knew nothing about her life, had no idea how normal people lived. Yes, his films were controversial, but in the end he was still a Savage. Society was forgiving with Social Register families. Ellie was part Italian, part Jew. No rebellion allowed. She hurried off to find Nicky.

Next to Nicky, on Talbot Coe's right side, was a remarkable woman wearing a man's white linen pants and a bow tie. Her name was Lucy Stone; she wore no makeup and had straight brown hair, dazzling green eyes, and an appealing sense of humor. When Nicky went to get another drink, Ellie took Lucy for a tour of the club's grounds. Now here they sat, in the stands above the grass courts on which Ellie had often played as a child. "Have you known Talbot long?" she asked, happy to be away from the Brahmins, as Billy called them.

"He and my brother work together."

"Is he a spy?" Ellie was getting drunk. She let her uncomfortable shoes drop onto the seat below.

Lucy laughed. "Anything's possible. As far as I know, he builds shopping centers."

"Billy Savage just told me my father worked on covert actions for the CIA. He says Talbot's a spy too."

"Nothing would surprise me. It's Mr. Newcomb's party, after all, and he was — "

"You knew that too?"

"I only know what my brother tells me. Simms wrote a book about it, I think."

Ellie sipped her drink. "So, are you a spy too?"

Lucy shook her head. "I have a gallery in Manhattan."

"Really?" Ellie sat up straight. She could help Kate if she played this right. "How marvelous. What's it called?"

Lucy twisted a gold and lapis ring around her wedding finger. Could she be married, this wonderful woman in men's clothes? "Stone's Throw. In Soho."

"I have a friend who paints." Ellie reddened. "People must say that to you all the time."

"What's your friend's name?"

Ellie felt a dangerous thrill mentioning her lover's name here. "Kate Paine."

"Kate Paine?" Lucy's expression changed.

"You've heard of her?"

Lucy glanced at the valet parking boys. "Didn't she do the lesbian couples book? The photographs?"

Ellie nodded.

"I love that book. We don't do photography, but if we did..."

Ellie lit a cigarette. "She's painting now. Full-time. Having a show in October."

"Really?" Lucy seemed genuinely excited. "Where?"

"San Francisco." Who would have believed that here at the Piping Rock Club Ellie could meet an adorable woman in a man's suit who loved Kate's work!

"I should get your number," Lucy said. "I'd like to talk some more."

Ellie riffled threw her purse in search of a pencil. "We're going to Maine next week, but I can — "

"Where in Maine?"

"Northeast Harbor."

Lucy grinned. "I'm going up there too. On Thursday. My brother's rented a house there for the summer."

"Call me as soon as you arrive." Ellie turned around in time to see Nicky hurrying across the lawn. She picked up her shoes and grabbed Lucy's hand. "Nicky, did you meet Lucy..."

"Stone," Lucy said.

"Nice to see you again. We met inside," Nicky said kindly. "Lili, the old man wants to go home."

"Call me," Ellie said quietly. "It's the only Sereno in the Mount Desert phone book."

Ellie surveyed the swimming pool and the new tennis courts. "Why don't we drop your parents off and do something ourselves?"

Nicky opened the driver's door. "I'll drive, Dad."

"I'm fine," slurred his father, not moving from the driver's seat.

Nicky's stepmother slid closer to her husband, looking dismayed. "Will, let Nick drive. You're — "

"Damn it, Helen, I'm fine. We're five minutes from home."

Nicky opened the back door.

"Lovely party," Helen said.

Mr. Webster's face was far redder than it had been when they'd arrived. "Took forever to get a drink."

"Was that Billy Savage I saw you talking to?" Helen turned to Ellie.

"He's making a new movie." Ellie had momentarily forgotten Billy Savage in the excitement of meeting Lucy Stone. "On the OSS."

"I suppose the little Commie will expose the OSS now." Mr. Webster was weaving, driving on the left side of Chicken Valley Road.

"His mother and I went to Farmington together. She was president of the drama club. And very artistic." Mrs. Webster paused. "Darling, you're weaving. Let Nicky drive."

"I'm fine." Mr. Webster gripped the wheel defiantly.

"His great-grandfather was Senator Savage from New York."

"Congressman Savage," Mr. Webster roared. He was headed right for a truck.

"Dad!"

They skidded across the road. When the car came to a halt, they were in a ditch by the trees. The truck roared on.

"Damn it to hell," cursed Mr. Webster.

"Everybody okay?" Mrs. Webster's voice was calm. "Anybody hurt?"

Ellie had rolled to her right, onto Nicky, as they swerved. Nicky's head had hit the window.

"I'm seeing stars," said Nicky.

"I'm fine, I think," Mrs. Webster said uncertainly.

"Damn truck didn't watch where he was going."

Nicky's door had collided with the embankment by the road; it wouldn't open. Ellie got out on the left side; Nicky followed, unsteadily opening his father's door. "Pop, let me try to get us out."

The car whizzed and whirred at Nicky's attempt; he cursed loudly and sunk the car deeper into the ditch. Taking off her shoes, Ellie jogged the half mile to the Websters' and called Triple A. Then she drove the station wagon back to pick up her family.

At 3 A.M. Ellie heard a noise. She sat up straight.

Johnny stood over the bed. "Mom?"

"What is it?" Ellie covered her breasts.

"Simon's sick, and we need seventy-five dollars."

"What?" Exhausted, Ellie forced herself out of bed.

"The taxi's waiting for the money."

Ellie shook her husband. "Get up, Nicky. We need seventy-five dollars."

Nicky groaned. "Can't you handle it?"

"He's your son too."

Nicky didn't move. Ellie grabbed his wallet, tiptoeing down the stairs, where an Indian man in a blue turban was standing in the hallway. Ellie handed him a hundred dollars.

Simon was sitting in the boys' bathroom, arms cradling the toilet bowl.

"Si? What happened."

"I'm fucked-up," Simon moaned.

Ellie sat and rubbed her son's back as he threw up into the toilet. When he was able to stand, she helped him take off his clothes, down to his undershorts, and put him in the bathtub.

"What happened?"

He didn't answer.

"Si?"

He was almost crying. "We went to a club in the Village and met some girls. They all love Johnny."

"Who does?"

"Everybody. The baby-sitter. Our friends. Strangers in some stupid club."

"I love you," Ellie said. Her boys had come home in this state because their father had lost them on his trip to the city. He barely seemed to notice he had children. Simon was half sobbing, half heaving. Seeing how hard it was for her son to cry, Ellie felt her own tears streaking down her cheeks.

Chapter **12**

Stretching luxuriously beneath the eiderdown that protected her from the foggy Maine morning, Ellie sighed with contentment, relieved that her husband was now a continent away. As the waves beat against the granite rocks below, she reread her last letter from Kate, handwritten, containing Kate's assurance that she hadn't given up on Ellie because of her "complications."

Ellie gazed happily around the white-painted bedroom that looked out over the Cranberry Isles. If the people from Los Angeles bought Nicky's mine — and it looked like they might — he'd promised to give her $100,000 right up front. It would be money to spend any way she wanted. She closed her eyes, thinking of the trip she would take with Kate to Mexico or Kauai, where they would lie on the beach, bake together in the sun, snorkel along the reefs, listen to the rustle of the palm trees, eat mangoes and drink margaritas — all alone, no children, no Nicky, no in-laws. It would be Ellie's reward to herself for maintaining her marriage, for taking good care of her boys, for getting them all through this vacation. And Nicky wouldn't mind; he was used to her vacations with women friends.

The white wainscotted walls and sweet blue-check curtains, so simple, so familiar, touched her this morning. She wished

Kate were here, lying with her on these freshly laundered cotton sheets, enjoying the vase of Queen Anne's lace and bachelor's buttons and black-eyed Susans her mother had arranged in the blue porcelain pitcher on her white pine bureau.

How odd, she thought now, that she had forgotten so much about her long-ago weekend in New York with Kate. Was it shame? Fear? Had it meant too little or too much?

This morning, comforted by the sound of the surf below, Ellie remembered that small hotel room on the eleventh floor of the Hotel Madison, near Times Square. The rendezvous had really been more for Kate's benefit than her own, hadn't it?

Of course, she'd been attracted to Kate, found her funny and surprising and smart, as everyone did at school. But until the trip to New York, she'd never assigned any great importance to their talks after hockey practice or Kate's eagerness to chat with her in the locker room. They had both signed up for the Chevy Chase Club trip to the U.S. Open at Forest Hills with girls in their own class. But they'd ended up sitting next to each other on the bus to New York, laughing and talking about sports and art and music and movies.

During that ride Ellie had felt herself opening to Kate in an odd, magical way. Kate was original and independent, was more bohemian and less conventional than most Miss Downey's girls, perhaps, Ellie thought, because her father worked in the newspaper business, wrote a nature column for *The Washington Post,* and her mother was from Mississippi, very literary and eccentric.

Kate had flabbergasted her at dinner with her unusual request.

"You want to kiss me?" Ellie laughed, looking at Mrs. Woodward, one of the chaperons, to be sure she hadn't heard. "You won't like it." Ellie tried to sound matter-of-fact.

"I won't? How do you know."

"I just know. Kissing is overrated."

Kate wasn't convinced, and her expression, so sweet and adoring, gave Ellie an idea. They'd get their own room, away from their classmates. "Then I'll give you a demonstration," Ellie explained. Kate was thrilled. The secrecy, the outlaw plot to rent their own room excited Ellie.

They'd lain on the bed for hours, fully dressed. Feeling suddenly very shy, Ellie put off the demonstration as long as possible. Still, the topic keep veering toward — what had they called lesbianism then? — pansies? Homos? They talked about Miss Krebbs and Miss Doolittle, teachers from school, who owned a house together on the Chesapeake Bay. They lived there in the summer and escaped there almost every weekend during the school year. And then there was Miss Mansfield, the hockey coach who wore madras Bermuda shorts and neatly ironed men's shirts from Brooks Brothers, who patted their behinds before varsity games and always had the sweetest smile on her face when Miss Metcalfe, the tennis coach and ninth-grade history teacher, was around.

Finally they undressed, put on their nightgowns, and turned out the lights. Ellie couldn't remember exactly how she began the kissing demonstration. But she did remember that when her lips touched Kate's and they lay in each other's arms tentatively exploring each other's bodies, she felt a roar in her womb unlike anything she'd felt making out with Nicky or anyone else. Amazingly she didn't yet understand about orgasms, didn't realize that if she and Kate had kept touching and feeling and pressing, her body would have begun to sing and moan and contract in a brilliant explosion of sensation. Still, the night had been exhilarating.

"How can we pretend this hasn't happened?" Kate had asked on the drive back to Washington. "It felt so good."

"It was an experiment, that's all. Don't mention it to anyone." Ellie had been impatient and scared. Yes, the kissing had been better than she'd expected. But it would go no further, could be nothing more. The words she knew to describe the Miss Metcalfes and Miss Krebbses of the world — *homo, fruit, queer, pervert* — were bad, all of them. Ellie would not be that, not ever. She was going off to Bennington in two weeks, and Kate, she explained, must learn to keep secrets, to use protective coloring, as Ellie did around her family. "Be as many different people as you need to be," she'd told Kate. Their night in New York, she told herself, had been a small pleasure, nothing more.

A small pleasure, Ellie repeated to herself, gazing through the fog at the limbs of the tall pine tree by her window. How could she ever have thought that holding Katie Paine was a small pleasure? Ellie resolved to call Kate after breakfast, talk with her about that New York trip, apologize for her cowardice of twenty-four years ago.

Simon slurped Cheerios, cocking his head to one side. "Why did Dad go home?"

Ellie glanced at the swinging kitchen door, grateful her mother was out of earshot, one meal ahead of them as usual, already making sandwiches in the kitchen for their picnic at noon. *This family crawls on its stomach.* "He has a buyer for the mine. He went home to close the deal. I told you that." Through the fog she could just make out the green tops of pines on the Cranberry Islands. Johnny was reading aloud to them from the catalog of Saint Paul's School, where he would start as a freshman next month.

Simon twirled the gold stud in his ear. He was wearing an EAT NO MEAT T-shirt that was torn in the sleeve, baggy khaki shorts, and purple high-tops with no socks. At least he had some color in his cheeks instead of his usual unearthly pale. "Is the mine worth anything?"

Simon was goading her, aiming for a fight. But she was too happy about selling the mine and her tropical vacation with Kate to bite. "It better be. It's going to pay for your college education."

Simon studied her with his penetrating brown eyes. "You hate men, don't you?"

"What?" Ellie looked up from the Bangor newspaper.

"Chill, Simon," Johnny frowned.

Simon tilted back in his chair. "She likes you and Nathan," he said to his brother. "But she can't stand Dad and me."

"That's not true." Ellie buttoned her turquoise robe and pulled it close to her shoulders. "I adore you. I think you're a handsome, brilliant boy who is very rude to his mother. And I am very proud of you." It was true. This morning, at least, she loved all her family.

Simon rapped his knuckles on the table. "Why can't Dad come back here when he's finished his deal?"

Ellie wanted a cigarette, but Simon would give her a hard time if she smoked. "We don't know how long it will take, and we can't afford to have him flying back and forth across the country."

Clearing his throat, Johnny read from the catalog. "'Students interested in marine biology may spend a month in the British Virgin Islands on *Calliope,* a 75-foot seagoing schooner fully equipped with a research lab.' Far out. Mom, can I — "

"Si," Ellie interrupted, "I've always believed that men are superior to women. They're smarter, and they know more facts. I went to college so I'd know enough facts to be able to talk to men."

"That's ridiculous." Simon eyed her incredulously. "Men don't know any more facts than women."

Glancing at her father's brown morris chair with books piled high on the arms, Ellie replied, "Men always know facts. All men know the difference between the Bosnian Serbs and Serbian Serbs and the Croatians and Muslims, and I can't ever get any of that straight."

"Maybe Grandpop does, but he likes foreign affairs. But Dad doesn't know the difference. I bet if we called him right now, he couldn't tell you who's who in Yugoslavia."

Johnny looked up. "Look, you two. It's not all that complicated. After World War I, Yugoslavia was put together from all these different countries. For years Tito kept the country together despite the fact that the Serbs, who are Catholics, didn't like the predominantly Muslim Bosnians. But after World War II, Serbia took over part of Bosnia, and then later the Croats in the north broke away from Yugoslavia, which was largely Serbian. Then Bosnia wanted to break away, but the Serbs in Bosnia didn't want to because they were culturally connected to Serbia. So the civil war in Bosnia broke out when the Catholic Serbian Bosnians started fighting with the more northern Muslim Bosnians."

"Awesome," Ellie said, beaming at Johnny. "That's exactly what I mean. Men know more facts than women."

Si tapped his spoon on his knee. "Maybe you have penis envy."

"Get a life, Simon." Johnny slammed down his book.

"Actually," Ellie said, lighting a cigarette, "when I was a little girl and my body started to change, I was very upset. I think I wanted to be a boy."

"Why?" Simon's mouth hung open.

"I wanted their power, I guess," Ellie said slowly. "Which reminds me, we're having people for drinks tonight."

"I think I have to take my power somewhere else." Simon rose and started up the stairs.

"Who's coming?" Johnny sat up.

"Some Texans Grandpop and Grandmom are dying to meet because they're very smart and rich and they know Simms Newcomb, Grandpop's former boss."

"Are they like hillbillies?" Simon asked.

"Hardly." Ellie stacked the breakfast plates. "They're very rich. Wait till you meet them."

"What do they drink?" Mrs. Sereno emptied a tray of ice into a silver bucket. She had changed into a pale green linen dress, her black hair, with barely a strand of gray, swept off her high forehead. She had, Ellie noticed, enviably few wrinkles for a woman of seventy.

"Not to worry, Mother. I'm sure they'll drink anything."

Because Mrs. Sereno did not drink and her husband and

daughter sometimes drank too much, the cocktail hour was often very tense at the Serenos. But tonight, with the Texans' arrival imminent, Mrs. Sereno was upbeat as she arranged the blue cornflowers she'd bought after their picnic on Cadillac Mountain. Everyone, Ellie noticed, seemed calmer since Nicky's departure for California yesterday morning. She glanced at her father, a handsome balding man with a powerful chest, soft brown eyes, and an outgoing manner; he was pouring bourbon into his glass. "Just one cocktail, Mother. In Ellie's honor."

Ellie was glad she had done her eyes and worn the black jumpsuit that made her look thin. If Lucy Stone were to help Kate's career and make Ellie's last week of vacation go quickly, she must look her best.

Greeting them at the front door, Ellie saw that Lucy's brother was to die for, straight out of *GQ* in his navy blazer and tan slacks. Tosh, his wife, had the body of a racehorse, tall and blond, with an infectious laugh.

It was warm enough to have one drink outside on the deck above the water, looking across from the high gabled house to the reach to the Cranberry Isles. Sitting next to Lucy, with her green eyes and loose-fitting khaki suit, Ellie felt wonderfully free and excited. Nicky was selling the crystal mine, and they'd have money again, and her parents were pleased with the Stones, and in a week she'd be back in Kate's arms.

Mrs. Sereno was telling Tosh and Gordon Stone some of the local history, about the enormous Bar Harbor cottages built by the Biddles and Vanderbilts and Procters in the 1890s; about Reef Point, the house that had belonged to Edith Wharton's sister-in-law and literary agent, Mary Cadwalader Jones, that had survived the great fire of 1947 only to be torn down in 1955. If they'd already heard these bits of history, the Texans were far too polite to say so.

The boys, clearly disappointed that the guests wore no cowboy boots or snap-button shirts, carried no six-guns or barbecued spare ribs, went for a walk on the beach.

"Kate's thrilled we've met," Ellie told Lucy.

"Where's your husband?"

"In California. He's selling our albatross."

Touching the collar of her pink silk shirt, Lucy smiled. "Do they exist in captivity?"

"Metaphorically speaking." The fog, which had burned off at noon, was drifting back in over the Cranberry Islands. Ellie offered Lucy crackers and Brie.

"My brother was thrilled you called. It turns out they don't know anybody up here."

Ellie spread cheese on a cracker. Lucy was being diplomatic, she knew, for the Stones had many contacts, if not friends, on Mount Desert. But the compliment warmed her. "Your brother is the talk of the Northeast."

"Is he?"

Nodding, Ellie picked a faded red geranium blossom off the plant in the wooden box by the railing. "Because he's from Texas and he's rich."

"How embarrassing."

"Not at all." With satisfaction Ellie saw that her father was showing Gordon Stone his beloved telescope in the living room. "They consider him very exotic."

"Like the albatross?"

For an instant Ellie wondered if Lucy were making fun of her. But seeing her guileless green eyes gazing up at the bay windows above, she relaxed. "I'll give you a tour," Ellie said, guiding Lucy quickly through the doorway. "We'll start at the top." Lucy's perfume and perfect breasts beneath her pink shirt were intoxicating. "I'll show you a picture of Katie."

Leading Lucy to her third-floor bedroom, Ellie pulled a packet of envelopes from her bureau. Carefully she extracted the Ping-Pong picture Jamie had taken. Ellie sat on her bed and patted the space next to her. "Come. Here."

Was it talking about Kate or sitting next to Lucy that was turning Ellie on? It didn't matter. Lucy's leg touched Ellie's, her arm pressing closer as they studied the photograph. "Kate and I went to school together," Ellie continued quickly. "We had sort of a...crush in high school — she was three years below me — and we've recently...remet."

"Sounds romantic."

"Very." Ellie winked.

The sudden rustling of the curtain near the closet seemed to startle Lucy. Ellie reached for her hand. "It's just a ghost."

"Really?" Lucy rose.

Ellie missed the warmth of her leg. "A child hung himself in that closet," she said with intentional matter-of-factness, changing the story slightly for dramatic effect. "He comes back whenever I — " A cool breeze slid through the open windows as the surf smashed against the rocks.

"Do what?"

"Do something naughty." Ellie could see in the mirror that her face was flushed, her pupils dilated. She moved one arm behind Lucy so that when her friend turned to speak, their lips were inches away. Ellie stepped forward.

How delicious Lucy tasted, how warm her breasts, how welcoming her perfume! *Is there time for the two of us? What a treat that would be! Nothing to do with Kate, just a nice break from this family.*

"Ellie?"

From somewhere below came the sound of her mother's voice.

Lucy backed away. "Is she liable to come looking for us?"

"Good question," Ellie said, taking Lucy's hand in hers and leading her slowly down the stairs, stopping at the landing to kiss her a second time and long enough to feel Lucy's hardening nipple beneath her blouse.

Mrs. Sereno studied them skeptically as they entered the living room, where the group was gathered around a crackling fire. "Ellie has given me a tour and has told me about your ghost and shown me a photograph of Kate Paine, an artist whose work I admire," Lucy said smoothly.

Ellie winced. She had not mentioned Kate to her mother, who had heard about Kate's lesbian couples book and the fact that she'd taken her lover to a Miss Downey's School reunion. "You're a senior," Mrs. Sereno had said twenty-four years ago, when Ellie told her mother they were friends. "Leave the girl alone."

Gordon Stone shook Mrs. Sereno's hand. "I hope you'll all come for dinner at Cutaways and have a sail with us."

"We'd adore it," glowed Mrs. Sereno. She pulled a book from the coffee table and handed it to Tosh. "The best book there is on Mount Desert."

Ellie walked the Stones to their car.

"Tell Kate she has an admirer in SoHo," Lucy said, looking at Ellie with amazement.

□ Part III □

As Ellie stood before Kate in her black jumpsuit, holding two gardenias, Kate stepped back. For a month Ellie had been handwriting on a page, a disembodied voice speaking furtively from pay phones and the dark hallways of the East Coast's great watering holes. The real Ellie had bluer eyes, had longer, blonder hair, wore more mascara, and had a warmer smile that was both more tentative and more amused than Kate remembered. Her cheekbones were unchanged; so was her coloring — a rosy tan.

"I'll put them in water," Kate managed, heart racing with pleasure.

"Put what?" Ellie brushed a hand through her hair.

As Kate took the gardenias, Ellie's eyes fixed on the Ping-Pong painting — the two of them arm in arm after their game in Turkey Run. Inches from the easel, Ellie squinted, then stepped back, putting an arm around Kate's waist. "Amazing. How you take nothing and make it something." She turned and held Kate in her arms. "God, I've missed you!" The smell of Ellie's perfume, the warmth of her arms, the longing she had felt for so many weeks made Kate breathless.

"I can't believe you're here," Kate said.

Ellie was suddenly in motion, inspecting the room, picking up postcards and photographs, studying sketches and feathers and an ashtray from Orvieto on the mantel. Kate felt shy, as if she were fourteen again and seeing Ellie in the halls between algebra and Latin.

Ellie turned and faced her. "What have you done to me, Katie? No matter where I was, no matter who I was with, no matter how beautiful the house or enchanting the people, I couldn't stop thinking of you."

In the moments since Ellie had entered, Kate's house had changed, had been shifted and stirred by Ellie's energy and passion. Kate's eyes caught the cleavage between Ellie's breasts above the soft black cotton. "Where does Nicky think you are right now?"

"At Hope and Raphael's."

Kate could not wait much longer. Her lips touched Ellie's, her hands encircled Ellie's waist.

"Katie..." Ellie pulled away and sat down on the couch. Her expression had changed again. She looked somber and worried. Kate's heart sank. It was a look she had seen often on Gina, and it made Kate afraid.

"Shall we talk about it lying down?" Kate reached for her hand. Ellie was staring down at the bay, at the boats, at the palm tree island beyond the marina. The studio felt very hot. Kate heard a ringing in her ears.

Distracted, Ellie frowned at the Ping-Pong painting. "Can't you do something about my breasts?"

Kate was surprised. "What do you suggest?"

"Put something over them." Ellie crossed her arms. "Make my shirt come up higher."

"I like your breasts. Anyway..." Kate handed her the photograph Jamie had taken. "It's exactly like the picture."

Ellie glanced at the picture, placed it on the end table, sighed, then looked strangely into Kate's eyes. There were red highlights in Ellie's hair Kate had never noticed.

"Nicky's moving out."

Kate blinked.

"We decided last night."

Kate sat down, then rose to put on the teakettle. *Nicky's moving out,* she repeated to herself. *The other shoe has dropped.*

Ellie was smiling uncertainly. "The strangest thing has happened. Nicky is having an affair with my cousin's wife."

Kate stared at her, digging her hands into the pockets of her jeans. "I'm sorry."

"Don't be," Ellie continued. "She's not really my cousin anymore, according to Nicky, because she and Wink are almost divorced." Ellie twisted a strand of gold hair around her finger. "I was taking a pile of clothes to the cleaners last night, and I found a photograph of Danielle in his pocket. And I asked him why he had it, and after a long, complicated explanation, too ridiculous to repeat, he said they were having an affair."

Carefully Kate placed a mug of spearmint tea next to Ellie on the end table.

"That's why he left Maine. He went home to be with her. There weren't any offers on the crystal mine. That was all a lie."

As she raised the tea to her mouth, Kate realized her hands were shaking. "How do you feel?"

"I feel fine."

Kate didn't believe her. "Nicky's having an affair with your cousin? And you don't mind?"

"I do mind." Ellie's voice was detached, her face changing from flushed to pale and deadly serious. She cocked her head to one side. "We decided last night. Or rather, I decided. I told him to leave. And he said he would, and he's looking for an apartment in Palo Alto right now. As we speak." Unzipping her black purse, Ellie found a package of Merits and lit one. The smoke from Ellie's cigarette caught the sun slanting through the south windows. "I mind, and I feel relieved," she said slowly. "It pisses me off that after all I've put up with, he's fucking my cousin's wife. And he still hasn't sold that fucking mine."

Kate swallowed. "I don't blame you for being pissed."

"But," Ellie said quickly, "the good news is that now Mother will blame Nicky for the divorce and not me and my...lesbianism."

"Divorce?" Kate rubbed her eyes. "Isn't that awfully fast?" *Have an affair,* Stacey had told her. *Practice having fun.* Divorce wasn't fun. A marriage and family dissolving wasn't fun.

"We haven't had a real marriage since I fell in love with Margo." Ellie's eyes caught Kate's. "I want out." She looked tired now and sad. There were dark shadows beneath her eyes that Kate had not seen before.

Kate stood up, sat down. "You're not going to see a...a counselor?"

"A counselor?" Ellie said quizzically.

Kate felt suddenly embarrassed. She had made so many decisions with the help of a therapist that it seemed natural to her. "If you talked to each other, got some help, maybe you wouldn't have to get divorced. You've never really — "

"Sweetheart," Ellie smiled, playing with the collar of Kate's shirt. "I want to be free. I want to be with you."

Kate's shoulders tightened. *It's perfect,* Stacey had said. *She's married. Won't have time for a serious relationship. Just have fun.*

"Kate?" Ellie inched closer. "Remember me? We met in high school. My name is Ellie." Ellie's hand moved gently down Kate's spine to her waist, then to Kate's butt. "I thought you'd be happy."

"I am happy," Kate said automatically. She had known Ellie for less than two months, and much of that time Ellie had been in New York and Maine. This impulsive, sudden action shocked her. She wondered if Ellie had any idea what a divorce would mean — the loss of income, the loss in status, the pain and disruption for her children, no more elegant Ivy

League husband to finance her horses and houses and romantic escapades. And eventually, if she stayed a lesbian, she would have to come out. Tell her mother. Tell her children. "What about the boys?"

"I'm not divorcing the boys." Ellie squeezed her hand. "Tell me what's wrong?"

Kate swallowed some tea. The studio felt hot and confining. "You don't just get a divorce like that, Ellie. Not after sixteen — "

"Seventeen — "

"Seventeen years. You talk about it for days and months and figure things out and decide about property and houses and — "

Ellie laughed. "We'll figure all that out."

Was her confidence real? Kate didn't know her well enough to be certain. She watched Ellie watch the smoke from her cigarette rise toward the redwood crossbeams in the ceiling.

"You don't think it's the right thing, do you, Katie?"

"I didn't say that."

"It's over with Nicky."

Kate inhaled and took Ellie's hand. She couldn't deny that since meeting Ellie two months ago, she had imagined everything — traveling together, living together, moving to Turkey Run. But those were just dreams. Kate dreamed all the time, lived in the world of her imagination. Dreams didn't come true, not so quickly, not so painlessly. "I'll bet he'll break it off with Danielle if you tell him you want to work it out."

Ellie made a fist and hit the arm of the sofa. "I can't stand him! I don't want to work it out. Neither does he."

This has nothing to do with me, Kate told herself. *If they get a divorce, it is not my fault.* The irony of the situation, of her arguing on Nicky's behalf, was not lost on her. "I saw his disappointment that night at your house, when you stayed up with me instead of going to bed with him. He still loves you, Ellie. I know he does."

"It's sex he loves," she returned flatly. "Not me."

111

"Maybe you turn him on, just as you turn me on." Kate hadn't realized Ellie's marriage was so close to dissolving. Ellie had had millions of affairs and never left Nicky.

"You don't want me." Ellie stood up, stared at her own face in the Ping-Pong painting.

"That's not true." Kate wrapped her arms around Ellie's waist. "I do want you."

Ellie snuffed out her cigarette. "Then why aren't you happy?"

Kate wiped her forehead. "I'm worried for you. I'm concerned. You find out Nicky's having an affair and decide he's moving out and that you're getting a divorce all in one evening. It seems so impulsive."

"I'm tired of pretending."

"I understand that," Kate said. "But — "

"Nicky may need me," Ellie said coolly, lighting another cigarette, "but he doesn't really love me — or his sons, for that matter. He acts as if the boys are mine, and he just happens to live with them."

Kate inhaled. "These are the kinds of things you can talk about in therapy."

"Katie, don't." Her eyes filled with tears. She began to tremble, then to sob. Kate held her, relieved that Ellie was crying. Tears seemed more natural than this cool detachment. "I've tried, and I've tried, and if he's got a fucking mistress, what's the point? I want out," she cried into Kate's shoulder.

That's what Kate wanted too, wasn't it? To have Ellie to herself, to have the relationship she'd been denied as a girl, to live out her dream with her childhood sweetheart, with the woman who had haunted her for so many years?

Trembling, Kate led Ellie to the bed and held her in her arms beneath the green quilt. Ellie cried, became enraged at Nicky, cried again. Just lying next to Ellie electrified Kate's body. She wanted to undress her, kiss her everywhere, go inside her. But she was trying to be supportive and protective and patient.

112

"You're not breaking up my family," Ellie said, rolling over on her side, propping herself up with her elbow. "If that's what you're thinking." She kissed Kate's fingertips. "My marriage broke up years ago. I want to be with you."

Ellie was unbuttoning Kate's shirt, her fingers playing with Kate's breasts. Kate forced herself to speak. "What about Lucy Stone?"

Ellie's hand stopped moving. "Lucy Stone?" All the tenderness left Ellie's voice. "What about her?"

"You talked about her so much when you called me from the East Coast, I thought maybe you were...falling in love with her." Kate blushed, embarrassed by her jealousy.

"Don't be silly." Ellie kissed Kate's breast.

"I'm serious." Kate pulled away, leaning against the wall behind the bed. "Did anything...happen with her?"

Ellie shrugged. "Lucy owns a gallery in New York. If I pursued her, it was because of you."

"Did you pursue her?" Kate asked uneasily.

Ellie's expression did little to comfort Kate. "She wants to be your agent."

Kate laughed. "She hasn't seen my work."

"She loves your work. She's seen your book. She's promised to come to your show."

"Is she coming to see my show or to see *you*?" Kate snapped, regretting it immediately.

Ellie looked like a dog who'd been whipped. "It's going to work out, Katie. I promise. I thought you'd be happy."

Kate sighed and kissed the top of Ellie's hand. What if Ellie had flirted with Lucy Stone? She was here now, in Kate's bed, the sweet scent of her gardenias taking over the house, telling Kate she was divorcing her husband and wanted to be with Kate. "This was supposed to be an affair. A little diversion."

"Well, it has been. You forgot about Gina, didn't you?" Ellie smiled. Kate nodded. "So it worked. Now you have even more of a diversion." She unzipped Kate's jeans slowly. "Or maybe you prefer me married." Ellie pressed her knee between Kate's legs. "Maybe you only want me when it's convenient for you."

"I want you all the time," Kate whispered. "I just didn't expect you'd — "

"Neither did I." Ellie was holding down Kate's arms, dragging her womb, then her breasts against Kate's torso. "Remember Forest Hills?" Ellie's tongue teased Kate's nipple, then her teeth tightened on it. "Remember my demonstration showing you how much you wouldn't like kissing me."

Kate laughed.

"I'm going to demonstrate again. I want what I couldn't have at eighteen because I was too fucking terrified."

The weight of Ellie's body on top of her, knee pressing between her legs, reached so deep inside Kate that she felt her womb begin to contract. "Why the sudden change?" she said hoarsely as Ellie's fingers slid against her clit. Kate tried to hold on, to put off the explosion. But Ellie's biting hurt, then roused her more.

"I'm happy with you, Katie. For the first time in years, I'm happy," Ellie whispered. "Your art and your talent and your lean body and the fact that we fell in love when we were teenagers turn me on. I find you unbelievably sexy."

Kate closed her eyes. How much longer could she fight it? "We both need time."

"Is forever long enough?"

Forever. The word plunged into Kate, slipped between her legs into her womb, caressed her heart. She was falling into a fast, insistent current, her muscles shimmering. She could not move, could not speak. Ellie was letting her full breasts fall out of her black bra. Kate felt a new fire between her legs as Ellie drew her breasts across Kate's face, stroking Kate's eyelids and cheeks and mouth with their softness. "Suck me," Ellie whispered.

Kate's lips drew a breast to her mouth. Ellie moaned with pleasure, pushing her breasts against Kate's face, her pelvis moving against Kate's. Falling backward, Kate was being drawn to the edge of a precipice as Ellie's fingers sliced her open. Kate was on fire again, her skin prickly, alive, hot and cold, loose like a rug, like an elephant's hide, not even hers as they tangled together, wet and hungry, Ellie's fingers moving inside her, nearing the falls, faster, deeper. *Forever. Forever.*

"I want to do everything with you," Ellie whispered, hands kneading Kate's butt. "I want you to fuck me and suck me and go down on me and make love to me every night. I want you inside me and on top of me, fucking me with a dildo, and I want to be seven and you're my nursie playing in my panties in a dark movie theater. We're going to have the life we should have started twenty years ago. I won't put it off another hour." Ellie's breasts reddened first, then Kate saw a blush move across her body as she screamed and arched, and they fell together into the violent, pounding current.

The green quilt was a canvas raft, and Kate was floating on it, her deadlines forgotten, her fear of Ellie's sudden decision to separate from her husband dissolved. All night they slept breast to breast, dreaming of their future, marveling at their past.

"What time is it, my sweetheart?" Ellie could not see without her contacts.

"It's 6 A.M. Do you have to go home?"

"Don't say that." Ellie sat up, covering her breasts with the sheet. "I don't ever want to leave." She rubbed her forehead. "I just hope Nicky remembers to pack Nathan's lunch."

"Want to call?" Kate handed her a blue terry-cloth robe.

"No," Ellie said quickly.

The morning sun warmed the studio as they watched a quail family — Kate counted thirteen chicks — outside on the driveway moving spasmodically up the hill. From the kitchen Kate stared down at the morning sun on the green fronds of the palm trees on the artificial island. *Ellie Webster is in my house. She loves me and is looking out at my garden of petunias and tomatoes, and she is leaving her husband so we can be together.*

115

Chapter 14

Waves retreated and returned as the hot sand beneath their towels warmed them from below, the scent of bananas and coconut oil wafting from their bodies. Kate sat up, gazing out over the blue of Banderas Bay, at the vast ring of green, once an immense volcanic crater, that circled the water and opened at the bay's mouth. Above them on the cliff, Kate could hear the wind gently rattling palm fronds next to the house.

They had taken the Zodiac out to the Arches to snorkel yesterday; today they were on the beach, alternating between the sun and the *palapa* and the swimming pool up by the house. The sight of Ellie, sleeping next to Kate in her black tank suit, her body long and muscular and relaxed, made Kate's breath catch. Silently she leaned over, kissing Ellie's shoulder.

The lime drink left a salty, tropical taste on Kate's lips, which were cracked from the sun and the sea. How different this trip to Mexico was from the one she had made years ago, one cold January, when she lived in New York and had stayed in a cement room in Pie de la Cuesta, a tiny fishing village near Acapulco, where the plumbing didn't work and she and Harry, who was about to hitchhike through Central America, both had turista.

Kate did not want to waken from this dream. After three months of scheduling their lives around Ellie's children and Nicky's willingness to baby-sit, they had for the first time spent a week by themselves, here in paradise, at this villa in Puerto Vallarta that Jamie and Claire had loaned them for ten days. There were only four other houses on the private cove, and they had Margarita to cook for them and Jorge, the butler, to bring them lime drinks and guacamole and barbecued shrimp on the beach.

A motorboat passed pulling a banana-shaped raft behind it on which tourists from the hotel were straddled as if it were a giant horse bouncing across the waves. Kate smiled, grateful to be away from the December rain in San Francisco, where at this moment "Silent Night" was playing in all the malls and manic strings of multicolored Christmas lights lit up houses and stores.

They had arrived here exhausted — Ellie, from the emotional strain of the divorce; Kate, from her show, which she had taken down last week. It had been wonderful. When Kate had walked into the Wilder Gallery that October afternoon of the opening, she'd felt a chill of pleasure and amazement seeing her portraits hanging together in the two large adjoining rooms. The gallery was alive with the spirits in her paintings, and people loved them. She had sold twelve, gotten three portrait commissions — one from Jamie and Claire — and had the work reviewed favorably in *ARTnews,* the *Chronicle,* and several local papers.

For the first time in nine months, Kate saw Gina, who had come to the show, dazzling in black leather and her wild black mane. She had bought the jungle painting of the two of them. She confessed to Kate that she was too fucked-up and confused to be friends but that the painting would be the next best thing to having Kate in her life again. And that was fine with Kate. There was no longing, no remorse, no craving to have Gina back. Kate's obsession with Gina was over. For the first time, as she'd stared into Gina's darting eyes, she'd seen the dark shadows behind the bright facade, seen how vulnerable, nervous, and frightened Gina was.

Judith, Kate's old and most beloved friend, with whom she had moved to San Francisco years before, came with her lover, Maggie, from New York. As she'd promised, Lucy Stone flew in and had not flirted with Ellie, as Kate had feared she might, but proposed a show in New York next fall. Kate had liked Lucy instantly, loved her funny, smart, Southern New Yorkiness, felt elated by Lucy's eagerness to represent her in New York. Ellie, who had raved about Lucy in the summer, focused all her attention on Kate, standing by her side, helping her with names, bringing her Perrier, and cheering her on.

Claire and Jamie had commissioned a portrait and had offered Kate and Ellie their house when Kate confided to them the nature of her relationship with Ellie.

"I'm very happy, my love." Ellie lifted up, holding her bathing suit over her breasts as she did. Sand covered her flushed cheeks; her hair was pulled back in a ponytail. Her body was close to Kate's, her legs stretched in front of her.

Kate smiled. Behind them, up at the house, the pink bougainvillea blossomed chaotically along the wrought iron fence. "This place is magical."

"Thank you for bringing me here." Ellie was making a sand castle on Kate's foot.

A string of five brown pelicans glided across the waves, turned, then glided back in front of the cove. "If something happens to me," Kate said softly, "remember me when you see the pelicans gliding."

Ellie released the sand from her hand. "You're planning a tragedy?"

"When I'm this happy," Kate said, "I start thinking about death."

Ellie kissed her hand. "We can't grow old together if you die. We can't rock till we're eighty like Miss Doolittle and Miss Krebbs."

The words made Kate's heart trip. "Are you just saying that?"

"I'm absolutely serious. I want to grow old with you."

They gathered their books and towels and glasses and climbed the pale brown stone steps to the patio. The salt had made their bodies sticky, so they slipped into the turquoise swimming pool, where the water was cooler than the bay and fresh as lemons. They took off their bathing suits, sliding through the aqua water, leaning on the side of the pool to look out at the bay.

Upstairs they lay naked on the huge bed they called the bridal bed because the white mosquito netting looked so much like a long, gauzy wedding veil. As Kate touched Ellie's shoulder, she saw two women: the girl of eighteen — fast, glamorous, funny — and the woman of forty-two — sexy, weathered, beautiful. Kate lowered herself, brushing her cheeks against Ellie's breasts. She kissed the stretch marks on Ellie's stomach, wondered what it must have been like to be Simon or Johnny or Nathan, floating in her womb.

Kate's lips moved to the soft, salty hair between Ellie's thighs, loving the taste of sea and coconuts and sand. She could never have enough, never get tired of this body and this feeling. Ellie gripped Kate's head with her palms as Kate slurped her tongue from side to side.

"You make me feel too much," Ellie whispered. Kate kept licking, feeling her own belly turn liquid, then touching herself as she slipped her fingers inside Ellie, tongue playing harder. Her life was changing, expanding as her love opened her to this woman whom she had known since childhood. What had it been like to touch Ellie twenty years ago in New York in that hotel room, their bodies firmer, skin smoother? Kate felt her tongue so full of love that she wanted to reach far inside, into blood, all the way to her breath and her heart.

Images of bougainvillea, the brown tile floors, a boat trembling, rocking, swaying in the waves flashed in front of Kate as Ellie came, screaming, held by water, by the love, by the

119

touch of tongue and breath and heart. Kate would remember it all, draw this place, this woman, this bridal bed, this outrageous magic, a blend of day and night, of pleasure and color and release in a single moment.

The sun was sinking, the sky going pink, then orange, then blue as the lights of the mariachi boats blinked across the bay. Kate and Ellie lay side by side, sheet drawn over them now, watching it all, skin against skin, the distant music becoming a jumble of sound and sight — the long bay promenade in town, the shopkeepers and their carved wooden fish, the smell of tortillas.

"When will you live with me?" Ellie said softly.

"You're not divorced," Kate smiled.

"That could take months."

Kate stroked Ellie's hair, which was lighter from the sun. "I want you to be sure."

Ellie sat up, her breasts uncovered. "I *am* sure."

"You're afraid too." Kate kissed one breast.

Ellie looked away. "I don't want to be poor."

"I know."

"I want to keep the house and my horses."

"What about the crystal mine? Won't there be money from that?"

"Even if he does sell it, it's not worth squat, the lawyer says. All this time he's led me to believe he would get a million for it. I don't have to sell the house yet. Not for two years at least, Nicky says, because he wants Nathan and Si to have a nice place to live. But in two years he says we'll have to sell it. If you come live with me, maybe I won't have to."

They ate pineapple that Margarita had sliced. They could smell shrimp and rice and green peppers cooking in the kitchen. Kate tried to imagine what it would be like to live with Ellie and Simon and Nathan. "I'm not ready to live with a teenager. And I'm sure Johnny and Si aren't ready for me." It would be hard enough when Johnny came home from school for Christmas. When he visited at Thanksgiving, Kate's backpack, with wallet and credit cards, had been stolen from the house. It had made her feel unwanted and angry.

And Simon needed time to get used to the idea of the divorce. The night she had met Ellie and Simon at Stanford, when they'd gone to a play for Simon's English class, Simon had been abrupt and withdrawn and hostile to his mother and Kate. He had left the play at intermission and disappeared. He came back to Turkey Run at 2 A.M., stoned, saying he'd run into a friend and they'd gone to Café Roma on University. Another night, a weekend when Kate had stayed at Ellie's, Simon had taken Ellie's car at 1 A.M., driven to Sunnyvale, and been stopped by the highway patrol for driving without a license.

"Simon's going back to boarding school next year," Ellie said, sensing Kate's apprehension. "I can't have him at home anymore."

"Maybe then," Kate said. "Maybe in the fall."

Ellie held Kate's hand. "I don't want to lose you the way I did before."

"You won't lose me." Kate stood up on the tile floor, turned off the overhead fan, and looked out at the dark bay. The sun had set, and a mariachi boat, white lights strung in a graceful arch from the masts, was heading back to the town of Puerto Vallarta. "It all seems so easy here without the boys."

"What would they say at Miss Downey's?"

"About us?" Kate looked at Ellie, so fully hers away from her family, from fixing her sons' school lunches in her ranch house in Turkey Run. "They'd be jealous."

Ellie frowned. "Sometimes I wish I'd never had a family."

Kate held her tight, stroked her hair.

"Am I too complicated? Me and my boys?" Ellie asked.

"Complicated. But not too complicated." Ellie had changed, relaxed since last summer when they'd met. And Kate felt changes in herself. She was happier, more hopeful. Ellie gave her a sense of future, of possibility, of sensuality and constancy. For most of her life, that constancy had come only from her work.

After dinner they walked along the cobbled streets of town, browsing in antique shops, ordering *café con leche* and flan at the restaurant along the small creek that ran through town. They walked hand in hand, laughed at the men who spoke to them lustily. Kate told Ellie about Judith, with whom she had moved to California in 1977 and who now lived back in New York State, near Albany, with Maggie.

"Why did you leave her?" Ellie asked, stopping to look at some woven handbags in a window.

"Because Judith stopped talking to me. Really talking. And no matter how I begged, she couldn't tell me what she felt. And I fell in love with Emily, who talked all the time. She wouldn't stop telling me what she felt."

Ellie laughed. They walked toward the square to find a taxi. "Eros," Ellie said. "The things we do for it."

"Do you regret what we've done for eros?" She was still uncertain, still afraid Ellie was going to disappear.

Ellie stopped. "No regret about loving you. None about divorcing Nicky. But I don't like losing the dream. The white picket fence and all that."

They came to a jungle tree in front of a church, a strange white light shimmering up into its branches from below, turning it into a ghost. "I'd like to take your picture here."

Ellie stood patiently while Kate took her camera from her backpack and studied the light.

"Why do you paint when it's such hard work?" Ellie said, her white dress even whiter against the jungle tree.

"I like making a mess."

"I'm serious."

Kate thought of all the years in art school, the bullpen at Doubleday, the illustration jobs, her photography. "I like to remember things, I guess. And honor them. When I paint someone or draw them or take their picture, it's like keeping a scrapbook."

"Is that why you painted Gina?"

"Probably." Kate stared at the waxy leaves of the jungle

tree. "I used to think I could bring her back to life by painting her."

"She's not dead."

"She was dead to me."

The soft light from the streetlamp gave Ellie's tan angular face a beautiful pale glow. "I think I'm jealous of Gina."

"Don't be. She told me at the opening, she's too confused even to be friends."

"I know, but what if she changed her mind?"

Kate stared at Ellie. "You really don't know the answer?"

"You wouldn't go back because you love me."

"Right." They walked along toward the promenade.

Kate put her camera into her pack. "You said that first night in Turkey Run that you've never been without a girlfriend. For the past fifteen years. Who did you have when we met? Is there someone I should be jealous of?"

"There was someone, but it's over now."

"Who was it?" Kate felt her legs trembling slightly.

"You've met her."

"Hope?"

Ellie nodded, cocking her head to one side. "But it wasn't like this."

"Were you in love with her?"

Ellie rubbed her eyes. "I think so. A little. But it was never like this. It was a friendship, really, with occasional sex." Ellie kissed Kate's fingers. "The last time she stayed with me was a few months before you and I met. Nicky was away in L.A. or Arkansas. Someplace. His meetings finished early, and he surprised us in the middle of the night. Hope just popped out of our bed and slept on the living room couch. In the morning she drove home to Raphael."

"That would kill me," Kate said, making a fist. "To be replaced by your husband in the middle of the night."

Ellie paused. "Kate?"

"What?"

"If there's an earthquake, I'll have to go home."

Kate scratched her head.

"It's just...if I have to go, I have to go."

"Sure. Me too, for that matter." She turned. "Are you okay?"

Ellie inhaled. "It's that old feeling. It's that fear that the other shoe is going to drop."

"It has dropped. And you're okay. We're both okay."

"Thank you, my sweet." Ellie kissed Kate's neck. "You're very patient with me."

"I'm very happy with you. I can't get enough of you."

"You never will," Ellie whispered.

Kate shivered. It was colder, time to return to the house. "Do you think," she began slowly, "we should stop?"

"What?"

"Maybe we should just thank the Goddess for introducing us and stop now, while we still can. At least we can salvage a friendship out of it."

The full moon appeared suddenly. "It wouldn't work," Ellie said in a strange, hard voice. "I don't have time in my life for a friend. I don't want another friend."

Kate blinked. Ellie's answer was not what she'd expected. "In that case," Kate said nervously, "we'll have to be lovers."

The full moon made their faces white, then disappeared behind a cloud.

A taxi pulled in front, and they got in. "It's not too late, Ellie. I'm sure Nicky would take you back."

Ellie shook her head. "I don't want him back. And he doesn't want me. He's happy with Danielle. She likes to fuck," Ellie said coldly. "I certainly didn't."

"Do you miss him?"

The taxi driver turned around, saw that they were holding hands, shook his head.

"Never," she said quickly.

On the terrace just beyond the living room, which was open to the air and covered with a huge *palapa,* they looked out at the bay. Kate could feel the waves relax and deepen her breathing. Her molecules were being reassembled by the Tropics, by the water, the coconuts, the balmy air, the sense of possibility.

"What if we moved here?" Kate said dreamily.

"To Mexico?"

Kate nodded. "It would be so much cheaper. It would take so much less to live."

Ellie was quiet for a long time. "Could we live by the ocean and swim every day? I could have a horse. And play the guitar again. And write songs. I want to write, Katie."

"Sure," Kate said. "You can write songs, and I'll paint."

"And we could afford to have an attendant for Nathan. So I wouldn't have to put him in an institution. Labor is much cheaper here."

"A big house with room for the boys when they want to visit and an attendant for Nathan."

Ellie was smiling. "I like it, Katie. It fills me with hope."

The next day and the day after that and all the days until they left, they planned their life in Mexico as they swam in Banderas Bay and took a ferry to Yelapa and flew to heaven parasailing and ate *camarónes* on the terrace by the palms and lay in their wedding bed, remembering their childhood love, climbing in and out of each other like happy puppies. They would grow old together in Mexico, making up for the twenty years they'd spent apart.

Chapter 15

"I told the boys," Ellie said over the phone on a rainy morning in late March. Kate was painting Mexico — the aqua pool and pink bougainvillea at the house — from a drawing she had made on their vacation. It was Kate's defense against the long rain this winter and a way to extend their extraordinary honeymoon. Once they returned home, the realities of Ellie's life — Simon's failing grades at school, the divorce, real estate school, financial fears — seemed to dominate both their lives.

"Told them what?" Kate asked, cradling the receiver as she worked on the white streams of sun cracking the surface of the water.

"That we're lovers."

Relieved but nervous, Kate felt her stomach tighten. Would it be more awkward for her now when she was with the boys? Johnny would be going back to school after Easter vacation, but Simon was there all the time. Could she be more open when she stayed with Ellie in Turkey Run? "What'd they say?"

"Simon went into his room and closed the door and played the Grateful Dead. Johnny said he already knew and asked me not to do anything embarrassing in front of his friends."

"How'd he know?" Kate asked. Of course, her sleeping in Ellie's bed when she came down on weekends must have made them wonder, but Ellie insisted the boys were used to that, that she often slept with friends when Nicky wasn't there, and it meant nothing to them.

"I think Nicky told him."

"And that was it?" Kate's hands were cold from the damp cottage, which had only one small heater. She pulled on a sweatshirt over the jean shirt she wore for painting.

"My mother wasn't quite as charitable. She says I've gone to Sodom and Gomorrah."

Kate inhaled quickly. "You've been busy." As a child she had known Ellie's mother, seen her in the car-pool line and at hockey and tennis and basketball games. She was a quiet, dark, handsome woman, polite but distant, who rarely spoke to the other mothers. "Was it okay?"

Ellie's voice was tight. "She said she hoped I could control my sexual drives until the boys are out of the house so that you and I don't harm them."

"Ouch." Kate closed her eyes.

"And she said I am the most self-centered person she has ever known and that I have never lived by the normal standards of decency and that I should give it one last try for the sake of my children."

Kate ached to be with Ellie, to hold and reassure her. "I'm sorry" was all she knew to say.

"I know what she's going to do." Kate could hear Ellie lighting a cigarette, inhaling. "She's going to send me a new subscription to *The Daily Word* and tell her friends that Nicky and I are divorcing because Nicky's having an affair with my cousin's wife, and she'll never, ever ask me a question about my personal life again."

"Shit." Kate knew Mrs. Sereno would have reacted the same way no matter who Ellie's lover was. But she had hoped Mrs. Sereno might be happy that at least Ellie had fallen for someone she had known as a child, an acceptable girl from Miss

Downey's. Kate had been foolish to think anyone would be acceptable to Mrs. Sereno. "How do you feel?"

"I don't feel anything." Ellie's voice was flat. "Angry maybe, when she said your being a public lesbian would make it harder for me and my boys. I told her that you are the only thing that's keeping me alive and that you make my life easier because you love me and you're proud of me and you support my choices. And she said, 'Well, that's self-serving of her.'"

At times Kate was glad her own mother was dead, no longer hurt by Kate's choices, no longer quietly judging and longing for Kate to find a man, marry, have a family. She had a family now but not one her mother would have approved of.

"So," Ellie said crisply, already armoring herself, "as far as she's concerned, you don't exist."

Tulips and daffodils had burst through the earth, and the sun dried the paddocks, and the fields turned greener, then brown from the sun as the days grew long and warm. By June, Ellie's mother had resigned herself to the divorce, if not Ellie's lesbianism, and the boys seemed more comfortable with Kate around, and their life together was rich and full. Kate was meeting Ellie's married friends with eagerness and trepidation. Hope and Raphael told Kate how happy they were that she and Ellie were together, that Kate had enabled Ellie to accept her sexuality at last and have a *real* relationship instead of secret, desperate clandestine affairs. Ellie had completely charmed Kate's gay and lesbian circle of friends, including Stacey, who had come twice to Turkey Run for dinner, inviting Kate and Ellie up to her house in San Francisco. Their weekends together in Turkey Run filled Kate with optimism and energy.

Their routine was set. Kate drove down to Turkey Run on Friday nights in time for dinner, as Nathan was going to bed. She and Ellie and Simon, if he were at home, would eat together, rent movies, and sit in front of the fire drinking tea and hot chocolate and eating Popsicles. Kate had grown used to Simon's awkward silences and bursts of anger at his mother. Even so, Ellie said, Simon was nicer when Kate was around — less likely to yell when Ellie asked about his homework or his plans for the weekend. Planning in advance was important to Ellie but impossible for Simon, who, sadly, had very few friends.

As Kate became more relaxed with Nathan, she found she liked holding his small, soft hand as he sat next to her on the sofa. He couldn't concentrate for long on anything and was already too big for the red plastic indoor jungle gym Ellie had given him for Christmas.

"He's getting smarter," Ellie would say with a sad smile. He couldn't talk or read or write, only make laughing sounds or cry if he couldn't find his book or didn't want to be locked in his bedroom. His books were talismans: He turned them over and over and over in his hands until the pages fell out and the binding disintegrated and Ellie bought new ones. In the car he would sit quietly, restrained by his seat belt, and when he went with them to the supermarket, he giggled and lurched eagerly through the aisles, thrilled by the bright colors and rows of pretty things. They had to watch him closely to be sure he didn't push over the cans of Campbell's soup, for whose red-and-white labels he had an inexplicable fondness.

Sometimes on Saturday the three of them would eat hamburgers at Jacques Dans La Boîte, as Ellie called the fast-food place in Redwood City. Nathan would throw french fries on the floor and roll his eyes and laugh delightedly whenever he saw another child.

Nathan's future weighed heavily on Ellie. She didn't want to put him in an institution, but she had no idea what she would do when the already tall six-year-old became a powerful six feet, three inches like his father and unable to care for himself.

Kate had even gotten used to Nicky when he came to pick up Nathan or Simon or something he'd left in the garage. Ellie was usually angry before and after his visits, during which he was very polite to Kate, asking, if he remembered, how her painting was going or if she liked living in Sausalito. Once he had invited Kate and Ellie to dinner at his apartment in Palo Alto with Danielle, but Ellie had refused. She was still angry at Danielle, although she swore to Kate she was glad Danielle had taken Nicky off her hands.

On Saturday mornings Mrs. Kwaznicky, who took care of Nathan on weekdays after school, baby-sat so that Kate and Ellie could ride back into the hills behind the house, canter up through the redwoods and bay laurels and out into the chaparral. Ellie, who believed that riding was a form of meditation, was teaching Kate in the corral to ride with her eyes closed, to allow her energy to move down through her pelvis with each breath.

"I feel stupid," Ellie said one night in July after she'd failed a test at real estate school. "Tell me why you love me again."

They were lying on the salmon-colored couch in the living room, the fire blazing. Simon was at the movies; Nathan was asleep in his little room off the bedroom. The house was different now, lighter and more peaceful since Nicky had taken his things — photographs of the Yale varsity crew, his tarnished silver trophy from the Thames Regatta, a painting of his father's sloop *Desire,* a heavy mahogany desk. Ellie had hung her carved masks from the Amazon, a painted wooden fish Kate had bought her in Mexico, and over the fireplace Kate's portrait *Mrs. Nicolas Webster and Her Sons.*

"I love you because you're funny and smart and you have children, which connects you — and me vicariously — to the earth and family and future in a way I can't be, and because you're sexy and you love art and we played field hockey together when we were girls."

"There are lots of lesbians who've been married."

Kate smiled, stroking Ellie's hair. "None that I loved at fourteen. None with a body that drives me crazy."

Ellie squeezed Kate's hand. "And we'll stay side by side in our rockers and rock and rock until we both die of blissful old age? Right?"

"You'll get bored," Kate laughed, leaning over to kiss her neck.

"Never," Ellie said, pulling Kate closer.

"We're having your favorite dinner." Kate had come down late on Friday night. The sun was still bright on the green lawn in front of the house when Kate arrived. Simon was out, and Johnny was in Maine for the summer, working for his lobsterman cousin, Wink, Danielle's ex-husband. "And then I have a surprise."

"What?"

"You have to wait. We're not telling her, are we Moona Loo?" Nathan chortled as Ellie washed red spaghetti sauce off his face and took him to bed. When she returned, Ellie uncovered two plates of crab imperial from Edward's Store in Turkey Run. "I have awful news."

"What?" Kate's heart thumped hard.

"The Van Landinghams invited Nicky to their anniversary dance at the Burlingame Country Club, but they didn't invite me."

"That's terrible," Kate laughed with relief. "What a slight!"

"It's not funny. I think Nicky's told them about my kissing girls."

"How many girls are you kissing?" Kate looked at Ellie, who had lost weight and was more beautiful than ever. Her hair was shorter now and straight and more brown than blond since she'd stopped streaking it. Since coming out and leaving Nicky and stopping drinking, she was happier, purer, softer. She could have her pick of girls to kiss, Kate knew.

"You know what I mean." Ellie grabbed a match to light the candles. "Is it so terrible to want to go to a dance at the country club?"

Kate found this new rejection hard to relate to. She wanted coming out to be easy for Ellie. She wanted her not to miss things as silly and insignificant as a country club dance. Kate put down her fork. "I know none of this is easy for you."

Ellie pushed up the sleeves of her black knit sweater. "It's so different now, Katie. Do you know what I mean? It's not even like last summer. Last summer was easy compared to this."

"What's this?" Kate sat up.

Ellie rose, put the dishes in the sink, made instant coffee. She returned to her chair and lit another cigarette. "I adore you, Katie. You're my best friend. I can talk to you about everything. I can tell you that I hate real estate school and that Simon's driving me crazy and that I'm terrified that I'll lose the house and I'll be poor and that you'll leave me and that I wasn't invited to a silly party I always hated going to."

"What's the 'but'?" Kate inhaled.

"The but is…" Ellie watched her cigarette smoke rise to the ceiling. "I don't know who I am anymore. For seventeen years I was Nicky Webster's wife and the mother of three boys and… Now I'm like all the other divorced ladies from Turkey Run, trying to tame a rebellious teenager, studying real estate, which I'll never be any good at, missing out on invitations to fancy parties because without a husband I'm not desirable."

Kate tackled the most immediate problem first. "What's wrong with Simon?"

"Before he left with his friend Jake tonight, he told me he wants to live with Nicky." Ellie swallowed.

Kate put down her fork. "Maybe that'd be good. Maybe he needs his father right now."

Ellie shook her head. "Nicky can't take care of a goldfish. He's too distracted by his business schemes. And Simon needs to finish summer school in Turkey Run, and Nicky's in Palo Alto, and it wouldn't work." Ellie put her head in her hands. "I'm beginning to think maybe something's wrong with him."

"Maybe he should see some kind of counselor."

"His teachers say he can't concentrate on anything. Just clowns around when they call on him."

"Get an evaluation."

Ellie slammed her fist on the table. "His mother's a fucking lesbian, and his father's got his head in the clouds, and his family's breaking up, and he's got a moron for a brother," Ellie shouted. "That's his evaluation."

Kate took a deep breath and cleared her throat. "I just want to say one thing, Ellie. The fact that you're a lesbian is not what's making him so strange."

"What is it then?" Ellie looked at Kate with desperation.

"I don't know what it is, Ellie. Maybe a psychiatrist — "

"I don't want to talk about it anymore."

Ellie carried candles into the living room. "Now it's time for the surprise." She unfolded a gray-and-red Navajo blanket in the living room, stoked the fire, and slipped a video in the VCR, lying down next to Kate under the blanket.

On the screen under the credits, a woman in a black leotard, black leather skirt, and black stockings was staring into a computer monitor while making a phone call. "Send her over," the woman was saying.

In moments a new woman knocked on the door. She was also in black leather and a thin black halter from which her breasts dangled suggestively. "I'm the office temp," she announced and proceeded to sit on the other woman's lap.

"What is this?" Kate scratched her head. "Where'd you get it?"

"I found it at the video store. It's called *Office Temp*. Try to like it, Katie."

Kate watched as the woman employer unfastened the temp's leather halter in preparation for her on-the-job training. Ellie's eyes were riveted to the red painted fingernails now stroking the office temp's hairy wet pussy. Ellie drew Kate to her breasts. "Touch me," she whispered.

Kate obeyed, unfastening Ellie's bra and taking a nipple into her mouth.

"Take off my pants," Ellie commanded softly.

Kate was amazed. She unbuttoned Ellie's jeans and felt inside her briefs. Ellie moaned appreciatively, fixing her eyes on the television picture as Kate played with her clit, moving her fingers side to side across her wetness. "Go down on me," she moaned. "Like she's doing."

Kate followed instructions, propping herself on her elbows, opening Ellie's legs, inhaling the salty smell of Ellie's cunt, sucking her clit, tongue hard and extended. "So good," Ellie said hoarsely. "So good."

On the TV the women were crying and barking like seals, but Kate could not see them, just Ellie's mons, where her fist moved slowly up, then back, up then back until she could feel Ellie's womb tighten and then explode as the women on TV panted and wailed. "Yes, Katie, yes!" Ellie called, writhing on the floor. In moments she was still. "Jesus," she sighed quietly.

As Ellie slept, Kate removed her hand and lay in the glow of the television considering this turn of events. It wasn't the porn she minded but the fact that Ellie had been more turned on by the impersonal women in the video than by Kate. Sex was so different for Kate, who was always hot for Ellie, always eager, always wanting more. She didn't need a dirty movie to feel aroused by Ellie. She was always aroused by Ellie, who felt like the Tropics to her, like a turquoise sea of pleasure on which Kate could float, weightless and ready.

Touching Ellie took Kate back to her childhood, through the classrooms of Miss Downey's, to the green playing fields and intense friendships, to Forest Hills and that sweet hotel room where she'd lain for an entire night with her beautiful, unattainable friend. Kate did not think Ellie felt the same way, and that made her sad.

Since Mexico, Ellie had been less eager to make love, reluctant and more passive. Stacey had suggested another vacation would help, get them away from the stresses of Ellie's life, from the children, the divorce, the house, and real estate school. Stacey was probably right. The pornography — so different, so removed from their daily routines — was a minivacation for Ellie that allowed her to feel turned on again. *Whatever works,* Kate thought to herself, resolving to rent films every Friday night until they could make reservations for the beach in Maui or the house on the cliffs of Puerto Vallarta.

Chapter **16**

In August, Ellie made up her mind to rent out the big house and move to the guest cottage in the barn. It was big enough for herself and Nathan, and she could make a ton of money that way. A boarding school in Vermont for teenagers with academic troubles agreed to take Simon for the fall semester. Ellie's parents, convinced that getting their grandson away from his dissolute mother would straighten him out, had agreed to pay his tuition. Simon had managed to land, then lose a job washing dishes at the local burger shop and seemed more and more miserable, blowing off his household chores in a battle of wills with his mother over everything from his music to his refusal to stay overnight at his father's.

One Saturday before Labor Day, while Ellie attended a real estate class and Kate was drawing by the corral, Simon came up quietly behind her and leaned against the fence, swinging the flyswatter he now carried with him at all times.

"Where's Mom?" he asked, looking over Kate's shoulder at her sketch pad propped against the top bar of the fence. Simon watched as she penciled the pink bougainvillea clinging to the far side of the corral.

"At a class on appraisals."

The pebbles dug into Simon's bare feet, so he moved from one foot to the other. "Do you think Mom'll be any good at real estate?"

Kate stopped drawing. Behind Simon on the rise was the red ranch house she had come to love so much. She looked at Simon's pale face and dark hair and huge brown eyes. "She's good with people."

Close by Nathan laughed, climbing the first rung of the fence, then stepping down, then climbing again, over and over.

"She says she's got to earn $60,000 a year so we can live here after the divorce comes through."

Kate pulled off her Oakland A's baseball cap and wiped her forehead. The sun was hot this morning; her shirt clung to her back. "That sounds like a lot of money."

Simon nodded. "I earned five dollars an hour washing dishes at the Turkey Run Café. How many hours would it take to make $60,000?"

Kate paused. "About 12,000 hours, I think."

Simon whistled. "How many days working is 12,000 hours?"

Kate did the math on her pad. "Fifteen hundred days about."

Simon shook his head. "That's like five years of washing dishes."

"A lot of dishes." Nathan ran to her, hugged her legs, threw down his book, and laughed. Then he climbed the fence again. He was wearing his tan shorts and a green Lacoste shirt from his grandparents; from a distance he looked like a normal little preppy kid.

"I used to draw," Simon said.

"Really?" She offered him the sketch pad and pencil.

"No way."

Kate shrugged. "Your mom says your new school has art. Maybe you can take a class this fall."

Simon groaned, rubbing his hand through his dark spiked hair. "I don't know about that school."

"What don't you know?" Kate looked up. She wanted him to go to that school, to get away from Ellie and be on his own.

"It's for freaks who can't get in anywhere else."

Kate kept drawing. He'd stop talking if she appeared to pay too much attention. "I thought you wanted to get away from Turkey Run High."

Simon bit a fingernail. "All schools are just major attempts at mind control."

Kate tried to conceal her disappointment. His going would be such a relief, an end to much of Ellie's worry and frustration. "The teachers at the Vermont school are supposed to be smart and really nice."

"They all say that." Simon tossed a stone toward the paddock. "All schools really want to do is to train you to obey the rules and support the status quo and get a job and never ask why the U.S. is always invading other countries and screwing the poor."

"True," Kate said, pushing her hair from her eyes. "But Ellie says that school in Vermont is different."

"Mom would say anything to get rid of me." Simon scratched his chin where a beard was beginning to grow. "Thing is, I'll have to go, because if I don't, I'll have to live with Dad, and that would suck worse than living here."

"Would it?" Kate said casually. "A few months ago you wanted to live with your dad."

Ruth, the neighbor across the road, waved at them as she opened the stable door and led out her gray Arab yearling. Kate wanted to draw that horse, with its curved neck and beautiful, strong head. Simon waved back. "Danielle's a nymphomaniac. One weekend when Mom was up at your house and Dad was here with Danielle, I came home from a concert with Caleb, and Dad and Danielle were like totally fucking on the living room floor."

Kate blushed, thinking of Ellie and the porn films they often rented.

Simon slapped at a fly. "I never saw Dad and Mom on the floor."

Kate began to draw the fence. "That's the kind of thing you do when you're all romantic and just beginning a relationship." She wished Ellie would lie on the floor with her without the movies.

"Well, it sucked."

"Yeah." Kate nodded.

"The folks have been married seventeen years," Simon said, staring off in the distance. "If they could make it that long, why can't they stay together?" Simon looked at Kate. "I know Mom's in love with you, and Dad really loves Danielle, but I still don't get it." Simon stuck his hands in his pockets. He had a nice body, tall and well-proportioned. "If I weren't such a fuckup, I'd do like Johnny's doing. He's never coming back here."

Kate chewed her lip. That was something she hadn't heard. "How come?"

"That's why he's working in Maine this summer, staying with my grandparents. When his job's over he'll go back to school in Massachusetts, and he says he'll keep doing that right through college so he'll never have to come home with Mom ragging him every fucking breath and Dad and Danielle fucking all the time and this family gone to hell." Simon paused. "Don't you think all human beings are basically self-centered?"

"Mostly." Kate rubbed her nose. "But not all."

"All the world cares about is money." Two riders in Western gear clopped past the corral on quarter horses. "Dad says Mom's never going to make it in real estate."

Kate kept drawing.

"Course," Simon said, watching the horses pass, "Dad's lousy at making money too. The sad part is, Mom's still counting on him in case she's a flop at real estate. She's really bad at math, and she says it's all math and reading these horrible long contracts."

Kate erased the lines she'd drawn on Monkey's haunches.

"You're lucky you've already proved yourself," Simon mused.

"I'm not so sure about that."

He slapped at a fly resting on the fence post. "You had a show, and you're having another one in New York. And you sell paintings, and the best part is," he said, sneaking up on another fly, "what you do isn't really work."

Kate smiled.

Simon scratched his armpit. "Do you promise you won't tell Mom if I tell you a secret?"

"Promise." Kate stopped drawing.

"There's about $10 million in the California lotto right now. Mom doesn't know it, but I took $150 out of my savings and bought 150 tickets. If I win, I'm going to buy the house for Mom and give Dad a million for his business, and then I'm going to buy a theater in San Francisco and do free rock concerts."

"Far out." Kate was touched. "Would you want a place like the Concord Pavilion or something?"

"Like an abandoned theater in the city that I'd fix up. Don't forget to draw the cactus." Simon pointed to the succulents on the far side of the corral. "My dad planted those."

"Did he?" Kate sketched one of the saguaros.

"Mom'll probably hack them down with her machete one of these days." Simon picked up a stone and tossed it across the road just as the black Rover came around the corner. "Here she comes," he said. Kate knew he was half glad, half angry.

Kate closed her sketch pad.

"Hey, you two," Ellie called, opening the back of the Rover. "Si, you didn't shovel the manure in the paddocks."

"Later, Mom." He started walking gingerly up the gravel driveway. "I don't even ride the stupid horses."

"At least carry some of the groceries for me, sweetheart."

Simon walked deliberately past his mother.

"Simon, please. Help me with these — "

He slammed the front door behind him.

Ellie dropped the bag on the ground and charged after Simon.

Kate followed. "Hey! Ellie!"

She stopped by the front door.

"Did you see these?" Kate held up her sketch pad.

Ellie glanced at the door, sat down on the step, then flipped through Kate's drawings of the corral and the horses. "These are wonderful, my sweet."

Kate ripped the sketches off the pad. "Take them."

Ellie kissed the paper. "For me who can do nothing, who can't even get her son to carry a bag of groceries?"

"We're going to grow old together," Kate smiled. "I'll carry the groceries." She put her arm around Ellie, both unloading the car, both counting the days until Simon boarded the airplane for Vermont.

Chapter **17**

The guest cottage was cozier than Kate had expected. By living there and renting out the big house to a visiting consultant from IBM, Ellie could make $2,000 a month, which helped calm her panic about money. The thick new carpets in the cottage, the fireplace, the low ceilings gave the place a sweet country feeling. The old sunporch was now an enclosed glass room with bunk beds for the boys when they came home on vacations. Carpenters had broken through the wall to the tack room next to the kitchen and converted it into Nathan's bedroom.

Although this place was much smaller, Kate was relieved that Ellie had moved from the big house, with all of its associations and reminders of her life with Nicky. Sometimes Ellie said the move was liberating; other times she hated her new circumstances, cursed Nicky, and blamed his financial failure for her loss in status and comfort. Still, she seemed to relax on weekends, when Kate came down.

Stacey rode with them often that fall, entertaining them both with stories about lesbians she'd met on the promotional tour for her new novel about lesbian relationships. Lesbian life was all new to Ellie, who, thirsty for information, pumped Stacey for details about lesbians' lives — how they fell in love, fought, came out to parents, had sex, broke up, fell in love again. Stacey liked Ellie, told Kate she was glad Kate had found someone so funny and beautiful and unexpected.

Phone calls from Johnny and Simon were upbeat. Johnny had been invited to join the poetry magazine, and Simon's roommate from Boston had invited him home for Thanksgiving. Nathan, cheerful and speechless, seemed to like his new digs in the tack room and wandered up to the big house only once.

As a consequence of Kate's show at Stone's Throw in New York, she'd been asked to jury several university shows, in Florida, Iowa, and North Carolina. Her work had been reviewed in four New York papers as well as *Artforum* and *ARTnews*. By next year, if she kept getting commissions, she would make enough money to share the mortgage on the big house.

They still fantasized about moving to Mexico, living in a house by the sea, painting and swimming and eating grilled *camarónes* and having a full-time man to take care of Nathan. But for now Ellie needed to be in Turkey Run to deal with the lawyers and papers and the divorce and real estate, and Kate wanted to be close to her gallery in San Francisco.

With all three boys at home for Christmas and Simon's moods black and threatening, Christmas was painful. At the therapist's, where Ellie took Simon in desperation, he confessed that he hated school, had no friends, and wanted to come home for good. Ellie insisted he finish out the year and made Simon promise to try harder.

By mid January life had settled down for Kate and Ellie. The boys were back in school; Kate had quit her massage job and was painting full-time, and Ellie had passed her real estate exam, signing on with the top agency in Turkey Run; she even got her first listing, a ranch house in the heart of Redwood City.

When the telephone stabbed through the darkness at 5 A.M. that February morning, Kate was sure a real estate agent was calling to tell Ellie about an offer on Ellie's listing. As far as Kate could see, the real estate business went on twenty-four hours a day, seven days a week.

Ellie lunged, knocked over the alarm clock, grabbed her glasses, and found the receiver. A long silence followed as she listened, frantically scribbling something on a Kleenex box with a pink crayon of Nathan's. "No, you can't... Because Dad's in Arkansas. Yes. Yes. Why on earth... Yes, I'll be there. I don't see why... I love you too."

Ellie put down the receiver and stared in silence at a long crack in the plaster on the far wall.

"What is it?"

Ellie made a fist, raised it, then slammed it against the mattress. "Simon's been expelled for smoking pot."

Kate's breath caught.

"He's coming tonight."

"Here?" Kate asked softly. For the first time in the year and a half they'd been together, their lives were calm.

"Yes, here." Ellie turned, her eyes wide and pained behind her blue-framed glasses. "Where else can he go?"

Kate felt an old familiar feeling. The complications of Ellie's life were a raging river that threatened to capsize them, sending them both sprawling over the rapids, struggling for breath. Kate could not imagine the four of them coexisting in this small house on weekends. "Can Simon stay with Nicky awhile?"

Ellie crossed her arms. "Danielle says no."

Kate touched Ellie's shoulder.

"I can't think about sex now, Katie. Don't even — "

Kate's eyes filled with tears. "I wanted to hold you."

"Sorry, sweetheart. I'm too angry." Ellie turned out the light and rolled onto her side. "How the hell can he live here?" she said finally. "I won't be able to stand it. *You* won't be able to stand it."

"I'm only here on weekends."

"You're going to leave me. I know you will." Ellie stood up and banged her fist against the wall. "Goddamn Nicky Webster!" She switched on the light, pulled on her robe, and left the room.

It was Monday, but Kate stayed in Turkey Run. All day Ellie talked on the phone — with the boarding school, with Nicky, with the therapist they'd seen at Christmas, with her parents. Kate bought groceries, made a pot of vegetable soup, fed the horses, and called Stacey late in the afternoon.

"Why don't you go home?" Stacey said. "Let Ellie and Simon work this thing out alone."

"Ellie's a wreck," Kate said softly.

"She'll survive."

But Kate could not leave now. Ellie needed her. Yes, it would be awkward, but it was only for one night. Two at the most. Thick and thin, that's what commitment meant. At midnight, while Ellie drove to the airport, she waited with Nathan.

When the kitchen door swung open, Simon nodded, his hair uncombed, his eyes bloodshot. He looked taller than his six feet, two inches, and pencil thin in black jeans, torn T-shirt, and black leather jacket. He dropped two duffel bags on the floor and opened the refrigerator.

"Not till you've put that stuff in your room." Ellie slammed the front door. "And send that leather jacket back to whomever you stole it from."

"I didn't steal it." Simon opened the glass door to the sunporch. "Is this my room?"

Ellie dropped her keys by the telephone. "You light one joint in this house, Simon Webster, and I'll call the police."

"Thank you, Mommy." The glass door shook as Simon threw it shut.

Ellie banged on a pane. "This is not a joke, Simon."

"Ellie?" Kate said softly. "He just got home."

"He's stoned," she hissed, turning back to the kitchen. She put on the kettle and lit a cigarette. "He's going to drive me crazy, Katie," she said, loud enough for Simon to hear. "He's stoned, and he's smoking dope, and he's ruined his life." Ellie dropped her elbows on the kitchen table and began to cry. "My little boy is a complete fuckup."

Ellie went to bed, leaving Kate in the living room, shaken by the scene. She rose and knocked softly on Simon's door. He was still in his jeans and T-shirt, lying on the bottom bunk.

"Hey, Katie. What's happening?" His voice was unnaturally cheerful.

Kate remained in the doorway. "How are you?"

Simon wiped something from his eye. "I'm okay." He was close to tears.

"I'm sorry about school."

"It's too fucking cold there anyway. It's like the South Pole or something." Simon brushed his hand through his hair. "Dad says I can live with him. That'll be cool."

"Did you talk to your father?"

Simon smelled of marijuana and sweat. "I can't stay here." Simon glanced at the bedroom door. "Mom and I...you know. You saw. She hates me."

"She doesn't hate you."

"Whatever. Don't worry about it."

"So..." Kate hesitated. "Welcome home." She tried to give him a hug, but his body was rigid.

"Did you talk to him?" Ellie's voice was a monotone. The room was dark and smelled vaguely of sewage from the septic tank near the house.

"Not really." Kate crawled over Ellie and sank gratefully under the covers.

"Does he seem stoned to you?"

"I don't know. His clothes smell like pot."

Ellie swallowed. "He was goofy when I got to the airport. Made a joke of the whole thing. He introduced me to some little Japanese man he'd met on the flight."

"At least he talked to someone." Kate touched her shoulder. "Ellie — "

"I can't."

Kate inhaled. "Not even a hug?"

"I can't hug."

The red numbers of the digital clock glared out at Kate: 1:35 A.M. "Things'll be better in the morning." She wasn't sure why she said it. She didn't really believe it.

In the morning Simon's eyes were so bloodshot, his speech so incoherent, his clothes, never removed, so disheveled that Ellie called the therapist, who called the hospital in Burlingame. By that afternoon Simon was sitting in a green nightgown, a plastic bracelet snapped on his wrist, in the dayroom of Burlingame Hospital's drug and alcohol treatment program.

147

Chapter **18**

The elevator doors opened onto the dayroom of the Burlingame Hospital Crisis Unit. Nervously Kate stared at its floor-to-ceiling windows, green linoleum floors, rows of brown folding tables, and orange vinyl chairs grouped around a television set, at which an older woman gazed vacantly. The nursing station was an island of activity in this room, to which Simon had been transferred two days before, when Dr. Veda, the psychiatrist in the drug unit, told Ellie that Simon had had a psychotic break. Her son was so confused and disoriented that they could no longer have him in the drug program; he needed round-the-clock psychiatric observation. His behavior, the doctor said, was not a normal reaction to marijuana withdrawal.

A small pale woman in her early sixties with limp brown hair and swollen eyes approached Kate. "Did you call my sister?"

"I'm sorry?" Kate stepped back. "I'm here to visit Simon Webster."

The woman frowned. "You promised you'd call my sister. It's Wednesday, isn't it?"

"Friday," Kate said.

A handsome African-American man with a shaven head and a gold earring smiled at Kate. "I'm Ron. I'll tell Simon you're here." He turned. "Judith, she's not your social worker. She came to see Simon." He led the woman to the television set. "Oprah's on now. She's having the Siamese twins today."

"I don't care about Siamese twins," the woman muttered. "I want my sister."

Kate shivered, remembering the hospital in Baltimore where her parents had sent her the summer she'd tried to kill herself. Psych wards were druggy twilight zones where normal social conventions no longer applied. *How scary this must be for Simon,* she thought, seeing him now in a green hospital gown and green pajamas coming toward her clutching a Mickey Mouse spiral notebook. His eyes were swollen, his skin splotched with red. He jerked back, then leaned forward. "Hey, Katie. What's up?"

His attempt to be cheerful made Kate's heart ache. She put her arms around his thin, stiff torso. "How are you, Si?"

"Cool. Good. Yeah. Nice to see you too." He looked hopefully at the elevator. "Is Mom here?"

"She's at work. I think today is brokers' open." Kate read disappointment in the sudden slump of his shoulders. "Shall we sit down?"

"Cool."

Kate tried to conceal her distress at seeing Simon so fragile and uncertain and in this bewildering setting. At one of the formica tables, Simon opened his notebook and held up pages of large, unruly handwriting. "I started doing the Twelve Steps, Katie. Back in rehab. It's all here." He closed his spiral, patted it, then opened it again. Kate glanced at his hands, which were trembling as he flipped through the book. When he found what he was looking for, he glanced at the nursing station. "Did Mom tell you about the aliens?"

Kate shook her head. "I don't think so."

"They've been watching me. Dr. Veda thought I was making it up, but when I told him about Granddaddy working for the CIA, he understood." Simon saw Kate's surprise. "They take orders from the CIA." He tapped Kate's hand. "You know about my granddad, don't you? He and mom had a big fight last summer 'cause he kept it secret all these years. About the CIA. Don't worry. They won't hurt *you*. It's me they're after."

"Wow." Kate didn't know what to say, so she tried to sound natural and calm. "Can you see them?"

Simon leaned back in his chair. "They put little microphones in the ceiling."

Kate glanced up at the white plaster ceiling. She wondered if the fire sprinkler system was what Simon meant.

"Not here. In my bedroom. This place is weird, huh?"

"The place I was in wasn't as nice. It was really old."

Simon's face brightened. "You were in a crisis unit?"

Kate nodded. "In Baltimore. When I was eighteen."

"Cool. Same age as me. I'm eighteen, right?" He looked at Kate expectantly.

"Eighteen. Right."

"How come you went?"

Kate noticed the black man at the nursing station watching her. "I wanted to kill myself."

"Far out." Simon sounded genuinely pleased.

A blond woman wearing black jeans, a white T-shirt, and black high-tops, with penetrating eyes and straight brown hair pulled back in a ponytail, shook Kate's hand. "Hi, there. I'm Suzanne."

Kate rose. "I'm Kate. A friend of Simon's mother."

"She's mom's lover," Simon grinned.

Suzanne didn't seem to hear. "I just want you to know, Kate, that Simon's going to be okay. We're going to get him out of here as soon as we can and back up to rehab on the fourth floor, where he belongs. Aren't we, Si?"

"Right." Simon's eyes rolled back in his head.

"That's great," Kate said. Was Suzanne a nurse?

"I don't want to interrupt. Tell his mother we'll get him out of here in no time. Nice meeting you." Kate watched as Suzanne moved on to talk to the pale woman who'd asked Kate to call her sister.

"Is she your counselor?"

"I think so." Simon opened his spiral again. "She's real nice. Says they have me on too many drugs." As Simon's head jerked back, Kate saw that his lips were swollen and chapped. "She told me to hide the Thorazine under my tongue and spit it out when no one's looking."

Kate blinked. "A nurse told you that?"

"Is she my nurse? I don't know."

Maybe she wasn't. Why would a nurse tell Simon not to take his medication?

Simon leaned close to Kate. "Mom says I, like, lost touch with reality when I was in rehab, but it was the Valium."

"Valium?" Kate was confused. She'd never heard of giving Valium to addicts in recovery, but maybe Simon needed it. Or maybe Simon wasn't telling the truth, didn't know what the truth was. Mental hospitals had a way of confusing people. Kate would ask Ellie about the Valium tonight.

Simon was pushing his pencil through the metal spirals of his notebook. "You've done your Second Step, right, Katie?"

"What?"

"In AA?"

"Oh, right." Kate was distracted by the odd assortment of people wandering in and out of the room. She'd like to paint this scene. If she brought her camera next time... No, mental hospitals didn't let you take pictures.

Simon propped his elbows on the table, holding his chin in his hands as if his head were too heavy for his neck. Then he leaned back in his chair and almost tipped over. "I feel like someone else."

"Are you Simon's mother?" called a cheerful, round African-American teenager from the next table.

"Hey, Leroy," Simon called. "What's up?" He turned to Kate. "Don't talk to him," he whispered.

"Your mom's pretty," the boy called.

"She's not my mom." Simon covered his face with his hands. "Don't look at him, Katie. He'll come over and start reading the Bible."

"Jesus is the Lord our Savior," the young man called pleasantly. "Drugs and alcohol are Satan's work." He stood up. "Did you offer the lady some fruit juice, Simon?"

"Oh. Right. Hey, Katie. Want some juice?" Simon rose, disappeared into the kitchen along the far wall, and returned with a small carton of apple juice, which he placed carefully with two hands in front of Kate.

"Thanks, Si." His effort to make her feel welcome was touching.

"So, what is this power greater than yourself, Katie?"

Kate looked at a meticulously dressed man in his thirties wearing a pin-striped suit and tie, talking into a portable phone, holding an expensive leather briefcase on his knees.

Simon followed her eyes. "Barry's a stockbroker." Simon began to rock back and forth in his chair. He didn't say anything for a long time. Kate waited. "Is Mom, like, really pissed because I got kicked out of school?" he said at last, tapping his hand on the table. "She thinks I really fucked up, doesn't she? I feel really bad. I really did fuck up."

Kate looked down at his notebook, at Mickey Mouse grinning on the cover. "Ellie wants you to be happy, Si, and to get better."

"She says I can live at home with her if I stop taking drugs." Simon ran his fingers through his spiked hair. "That won't be a problem now. I hate drugs. I was smoking every day at school." His brown eyes searched hers. "Was I really bad at Christmas?"

Kate swallowed. "Sort of restless and unhappy. But not bad."

"Shit." Simon covered his face with his hands. "I really let her down. I've got to make an amends to her."

Her heart ached for him. "What step are you on now?" she offered.

"Steps are upstairs on four, in rehab. Down here they don't care about steps, just drugs."

"Help! Nurse! Somebody help me!" In the lounge area near the TV, an elderly white-haired woman tore off her blouse and started slapping her skin. "Get these bugs off me."

"Put your shirt on, Mrs. Curtiss. There aren't any bugs." The black nurse with the gold earring hurried across the room, while the stockbroker in the pinstripe frantically pressed the buttons on his telephone. "Your daughter's coming at five. Put your shirt on, Mrs. Curtiss."

Simon cocked his head. "She's nuts. I think it's the shock treatments."

"I didn't think they shocked people anymore." Kate could not help staring. The old woman had looked calm and dignified moments before.

"If they shock me, I'll be pissed."

"They won't," Kate said reassuringly.

"What's your higher power?" Simon asked, watching the nurse help Mrs. Curtiss get dressed. "Is the Goddess, like, your higher power?"

"Sometimes."

"Do you hate men?" Simon looked at Kate curiously.

Kate chewed her lip. "I hate some men."

"Like who?"

"I'm not too fond of Pat Buchanan and Rush Limbaugh and those fundamentalists who want to lock up lesbians and gay men."

"That's fucked." Simon tapped his fingers against the table, then leaned way back in his chair. "Did your dad, like, molest you?"

"What?"

Simon twisted the plastic hospital bracelet on his wrist. "My friend Laura was molested by her boss." He pulled open his notebook and riffled through the pages. "I don't know what I did with her phone number. Do you have it? I need to call her. I keep forgetting. I can't remember things anymore."

The male nurse tapped Simon's shoulder. "Your group's meeting now, Si."

"Group?" He looked at the clock. "Ron, listen. I'd like to go off these drugs. They're affecting my brain."

"Have you talked to Dr. Veda?"

Simon stood up. "See, I should be upstairs doing the steps, going off drugs instead of taking Thorazine. It's fucking up my brain. I can't think."

"Let's talk to Dr. Veda about it tomorrow," Ron said gently.

"It makes my mouth dry."

"Water cooler's right over there." Ron pointed to the kitchenette.

Simon picked up his Mickey Mouse spiral. "This is my mom's friend Kate."

"Hello again." Ron shook Kate's hand. "Simon's much better today."

"Is he?"

Simon looked at Kate. "Mom's coming tonight, isn't she?"

"I'm not sure." Ellie had told Kate she'd rented a video.

Simon squinted. "What day is it?"

"Friday," Kate said.

"Are you going to the house now?"

Kate nodded.

"Say hi to Mom." He smiled and shuffled down the hall with Ron. From the back, in his green shift and baggy pajama pants, he looked like a scared kid, much younger than his eighteen years.

That night in bed Kate drew close and held Ellie tight.

"I can't," she said.

"Can we hug?"

Ellie did not turn over. "I'm upset."

"Seems like you're always upset."

"Wouldn't you be?"

Kate sucked in her breath. "Ellie, I know things have been hard. But does it mean we can never make love? You still turn me on. I don't know what to do with that."

Silence.

"Talk to me," Kate begged.

"About what?"

"Tell me what's wrong. Tell me how you feel."

"You won't like it."

Kate inhaled. "Tell me anyway."

"All you think about is sex. I might as well be married to Nicky Webster."

The words stung. Kate sat up. "You really think that?"

"I feel coerced."

Kate rubbed her eyes and turned on the light. "We need to talk."

Ellie stared at the wall. "There's nothing to talk about."

Just the sight of Ellie's breasts beneath her sheer blue nightgown made Kate's heart race. "Ellie, I love you. Does that mean anything?"

Silence.

Kate's heart pounded. "Have you fallen out of love? Is that what this is about? Should we take a break? Should we see less of each other?"

"Don't be silly." Still she did not look at Kate.

"I'm not being silly. I want to know. There was a time when you and I made love as soon as I walked in the door on Friday night. Now you act like I'm the enemy. I'm your lover, Ellie. I'm attracted to you. It's not wrong to want to express that love."

Ellie said nothing.

Kate felt scared. She had reached Ellie's wall, that barrier of anger and fear and silence that went up when Kate pushed Ellie to say what was bothering her. Was it the same barrier Ellie had raised twenty years ago when she told Kate never to contact her again?

"I hate my life," Ellie said grimly, staring at the ceiling.

Don't take it personally, Kate told herself. *Her whole life is falling apart. She's divorcing her husband, her mother says she's gone to the devil. One son is no smarter than a dog, and her other son thinks the CIA is spying on him.* "A lot has

155

changed," Kate offered, touching Ellie's shoulder. "It's going to get better."

"Nothing's changed." Ellie glanced at Kate, her eyes filling with tears. "I'm miserable."

Kate felt a knot in her heart. "Sweetheart — "

"I'm a fucking failure."

"You're not a failure. You've come a really long way in a very short time. You're recovering from seventeen years of an unhappy marriage."

"It wasn't always unhappy."

"Sorry. A seventeen-year marriage that was sometimes unhappy."

"And look at Simon."

"He's going to get better."

"I wish I could believe that." Ellie lay there for what seemed forever to Kate, staring at the ceiling.

"Do you love me at all?" Kate said at last.

Ellie reached for Kate's hand. "You're the only good thing in my life, Katie." She sank down into the bed, clinging to Kate. "I want to grow old with you," she whispered. She lifted her nightgown and put Kate's hands on her waist. "Force me," she whispered. "That's what Nicky did. If you force me, I'll get turned on."

"Force you?" Kate said, incredulous.

"Lie on top of me."

Kate obeyed.

"Kiss my breasts." Gently Kate's lips touched Ellie's soft breasts as Ellie put Kate's hand between her legs. "Don't stop," Ellie said as Kate became lost in Ellie's silver slickness. They moved closer, hips pressed together, Ellie wet and moaning, Kate horny and hot and desperate to obliterate the sound of Ellie's words "I'm miserable" and the image of Simon, pale and lost, locked in the crisis unit in green pajamas.

Chapter **19**

The late February sun shone weakly down on the palm tree island in the bay as Kate drank her coffee, waiting uneasily for Ellie's morning call. Maybe Ellie wasn't going to call. Since last weekend she had been brusk and distant on the phone, had asked Kate not to phone at bedtime yesterday, as she usually did, because she was exhausted and didn't want to be disturbed.

In the afternoon Kate would drive down to Turkey Run to spend the weekend and celebrate her birthday. She did not feel very festive with Ellie so withdrawn and strange. *Be patient,* Kate told herself. *Simon's illness is making her crazy.* When the phone rang, she relaxed.

But Ellie's voice was tight and formal as it had been last night. "Are you sitting down?"

"What's up?"

"I know you don't like bad news over the phone, but I can't wait any longer. I'm having an affair."

Kate stared at her sketch of Simon hunched over his Mickey Mouse spiral at the long folding table in the dayroom of the crisis unit.

"I have open houses on Saturday and Sunday. So I won't be around very much. But I'll take you out for dinner tomorrow night. We can go to that Italian — "

"Who is it?" Kate's heart banged in her chest.

Ellie coughed. "No one you know."

Kate could hear "Oh, What a Beautiful Morning" playing on Nathan's Wee Sing tape in Ellie's kitchen. Ellie had mentioned taking a walk with someone named Alyson, whom Kate had never met, but Ellie had said such unpleasant things about her — that she was rich and Republican and drank too much — that it had not occurred to Kate to be jealous. "It's Alyson?"

"Yes." Ellie's calm frightened her.

"When did it start?"

"Monday."

Kate inhaled. "I'll come down now."

Ellie hesitated. "I have some things I need to do at the office."

Kate rubbed her eyes. "Isn't this more important than your office?"

"I'll hurry," Ellie said. "I'll meet you at the house at noon." She paused. "At 3 P.M. I meet with Simon's doctor."

"How could you?" Kate said, her hands trembling.

Ellie's voice was almost a whisper. "At least I'm telling the truth."

She is having an affair. The words thundered through Kate's chest and made ghosts of her bones. Five days ago, on Monday, the same day Ellie had started the affair, she had told Kate she wanted to grow old with her.

Kate's house looked suddenly unreal. The paintings were somebody else's, her body felt heavy and unfamiliar. The coffeepot, her feet, the view of the bay were dream images. She knew what Simon must have felt when he was going crazy.

She called Stacey. "Ellie is having an affair."

"What happened?"

"She's been weird all week. Cold and bitchy."

Stacey's voice was gentle. "Who is it?"

"Some woman named Alyson who's rich and owns a catering company in Menlo Park."

158

"It's the stress, Katie. It's like an alcoholic in a slip. Don't make any hasty decisions."

"I'm going down there to talk to her."

"Now? Why?"

Kate was confused. "I have to find out what this means."

"If she's right in the heat of it, she may not say anything that comforts you." Stacey's voice was firm.

Kate looked up at the drawing of Simon. Was she, like him, to become another of Ellie's lost children? She had to go, look her in the eye, hear her explain, assess the damage.

Should she pack for an hour or for the weekend?

She decided to wear her black jeans, black Mafia shirt, and black leather tie. *I'm dressed for a funeral,* she thought, tossing her sweats and running shoes and underpants into a bag.

The drive south hurt. She had entered the land of the dead. What tape could she play to keep from seeing the betrayal, from imagining Ellie and Alyson making love? The music on the radio — love songs about romance and pleasure — hurt. Her body hurt; her head hurt.

As she passed Zim's coffee shop on 19th Avenue and the Air Force bomber in the children's park and San Francisco State University, she reviewed the past week. Of course Ellie hadn't wanted to talk on the phone; she'd been in bed with Alyson. This morning Alyson had probably been sitting next to Ellie in the kitchen, waiting for their call to end so she could find out how Kate had reacted.

In the town of Turkey Run, Ellie's big black Land Rover was parked in front of her real estate office. *She has not gone home yet to talk to me,* Kate thought. *She is late for our meeting.*

Kate parked. As she walked toward Ellie's office, the door opened and Ellie emerged in riding pants, sneakers, and a blue scarf draped over her black sweater.

"I'll meet you at the house," Kate yelled, turning away. She drove past the fire station and the elementary school, where

Nathan sat in class strapped to his chair. She passed the library, where she had taken out books on horses so she would know what kind to get when she had enough money to live with Ellie. At Ellie's road she turned up the hill, where the horses leaned over the fences watching the suburban ladies act out their domestic drama. At Ellie's by the corral, Isis, the big mare, chewed her hay indifferently.

Outside the guest cottage, Ellie hugged Kate awkwardly. The body which had always comforted Kate was now the source of pain. Inside the house neither knew what to do, where to sit.

"Are you hungry?" Ellie opened the refrigerator, her face looking tired and much older today.

"I'm not hungry," Kate said. She did not know what she felt, but it was not hunger.

Ellie pulled a hunk of Swiss cheese from the refrigerator, breaking a piece of white bread from a baguette.

"This white bread is good, but it has no taste," Kate had told Ellie last weekend, when the white bread first appeared in Ellie's refrigerator. "Where did you get it?"

"From Alyson."

"Who is Alyson?" Kate had asked.

"A friend of my manager's at work."

Alyson is white bread, Kate thought now as she stared at the piece Ellie was eating. "Is that why you like her?" Kate said angrily.

"What?"

"Do you like Alyson because she is white bread?"

Ellie looked down at her hands uncomfortably and sipped her instant coffee.

Kate went outside onto the deck, and Ellie followed. The earth was dry; they'd had very little rain since December. *I want to undress her,* Kate thought, staring at the round contours of her chest. *I want to rest my head against her breasts. If we could touch, all this might go away.*

"So," Kate said, "is this something we're working on

together? Are we trying to get through this as a couple? Or is it over?"

Ellie lit a cigarette and crossed her legs. "I love you, Katie, but I don't want to be lovers."

The geraniums bowed happily in the breeze; Kate felt a cord tighten around her neck. "It's over?" The blood was draining from her face as if she were disappearing. She could feel something important, something like her soul, leave her body.

"I want us to be friends," Ellie said tentatively. "I want us to talk and ride and do all sorts of things together. But I don't want to be lovers."

The sun seemed too bright, the earth too dry, the air too cold and then too hot. "But what about growing old together? That's what you wanted Monday. You said we had to stick with each other till the end because if we broke up, we'd just have to go through all the same stuff with someone new. What about that?"

Ellie chewed her lip, glancing up at the painting of herself and her sons. "When I announced my engagement to Nicky Webster, my friends said, 'Ellie, you can't get married. You're not monogamous. You can't commit yourself to one person.' " Ellie inhaled. "They were right."

Kate heard the words, but she couldn't grasp the concept. "You *have* a commitment to me. You've been monogamous for the last year and a half. You never complained. You've never said you wanted to have an affair. Now you're in love with Alyson? Just like that?"

Ellie appeared to consider Kate's statement. "I don't know if I'm in love with her. But I know I don't want it to end."

Kate paced the deck. Until this morning she was building a life with Ellie, planned to move in with her next fall. "Can we lie down?" Kate whispered. If she touched Ellie, if they could hold each other, Ellie would remember.

Ellie opened the kitchen door and walked slowly into the bedroom. The house was a mess. Daffodils were dying in their

161

vases. The rug had not been vacuumed; little white threads of lint lay on its surface. There were dishes in the sink. *Her mental condition is ragged,* Kate thought. *She doesn't know what she's doing.* This comforted Kate. *She can't change her entire life so easily. It's not possible.*

In the bedroom the pillowcases were gone, but the sheets were still on. Kate remembered Ellie's haste to change the sheets on Monday morning. That must have been in Alyson's honor. Today she had only planned to change the *pillowcases.* Were the Alyson-soaked pillowcases more revealing than the sheets?

They lay on top of the bed. Ellie was someone else. Her touch cut like a knife. Kate stared at the room as Ellie watched her nervously, protected from pain by her new romance.

Kate got up and wandered into the living room, sitting on the couch where Nathan always jumped up and down, up and down. Ellie sat next to her.

"Are you happy now that you've dumped me?" Kate said, clutching a cushion to her stomach.

"I'm relieved that I'm not lying." Ellie's eyes were bloodshot.

Good, Kate thought. *She is suffering a little.*

"Are you satisfied now that you've seduced someone new? Do you feel sexy again?" Stacey had told Kate not to make Ellie feel guilty, but she could not stop herself. She wanted Ellie to suffer.

"I'm not happy about hurting you," Ellie said, lighting a cigarette. "I still love you."

Kate laughed.

"I just don't want to be married to you."

Kate rose and went outside again to be in the sun. But she could not sit down, could not stay still. The sun did not warm her. Everything about Ellie was cold today. Kate looked at her watch. Soon Ellie would have to go to the hospital to meet with her son's psychiatrist. "Are you going to let me go so easily?" Kate twisted a Kleenex around and around her fingers. "Aren't you going to fight for me? Not even a little?"

Ellie stared at the daffodils on the hillside.

She wants this scene to be over, Kate thought. *This is not pleasant, this disposing of lovers.*

"I don't want to fight."

"Don't you have anything to say?" Kate stood inches from her. "You're finished, just like that?"

"I want to say...thank you," Ellie whispered. "For everything you've done for me and my family." More than anything, this thank you chilled Kate. Ellie was acknowledging Kate for services rendered. She was calling it quits. "I feel like I'm losing my best friend."

"You are." Kate rubbed her eyes.

"I'm afraid of being alone. But I probably need to be alone."

"Alone with Alyson?"

Ellie blinked. "It's all because of sex."

Kate stared at her.

"I thought it would be different with women. But you were just like Nicky, always wanting sex."

Kate swallowed. "You're the one having the sex, not me."

Ellie bit her lip. "I'm not being clear."

Kate reddened. "Ellie, I love you. It would be strange if I didn't want to have sex with you."

Ellie crushed out her cigarette. "Surely this isn't a surprise. Couldn't you see it coming?"

"On Monday we were going to grow old together." Kate was starting to cry. "How could I see it coming?"

Ellie took her hand. "Sweetheart, I have to go to the hospital at 3. Nathan and the baby-sitter are coming in fifteen minutes. Stay here. I'll pick up something for dinner at Edward's, and we can rent a movie."

"Nathan and the baby-sitter are coming?"

"You can close the bedroom door. Take a nap if you want."

"Right." Kate looked at the house that she had helped Ellie remodel. "It's her house now."

"It's *my* house," Ellie said flatly.

Kate looked for signs of Alyson. She saw records on top of the stereo. "Is this what you and Alyson have been listening

163

to?" She held up the album cover of Ravel's "Bolero," then threw the jacket across the living room, hitting the Mexican wooden fish she had given Ellie in Puerto Vallarta. The fish crashed to the ground.

"Kate, please" was all Ellie said. She was waiting for this to be over so she could call Alyson.

"This is your love nest with Alyson now." Kate banged out of the kitchen onto the deck, eyes stopped by the red canvas deck chairs she had given Ellie for Christmas. She lifted one and hurled it over the side of the deck onto the green ravine below. She liked doing that. *These are my fucking chairs,* she thought. *I gave them to her. I can throw them away.* Ellie stood in the doorway watching as Kate threw each chair over the side of the deck. "Fuck you!" Kate yelled. "Fuck you!"

Back in the house Kate pulled the receiver off the telephone. "The telephone is the instrument of betrayal." She slammed it down, walked into the bedroom, and threw herself on the bed. She stuffed a pillow against her stomach. Ellie stood in the doorway.

"Why didn't you tell me? Why didn't you warn me that you were unhappy? Why didn't you let me know that other people were turning you on?"

"I didn't know," Ellie said softly, "until it happened."

Kate fell onto the floor into the space between the bed and the window, the place where she left her canvas tote each weekend, next to the ex-husband's bureau and the straw laundry basket. She screamed. She screamed until she began to sob and then to choke. She was losing her lover, whom she had known since childhood.

Ellie handed Kate a soggy gray towel with a conch shell patterned into the weave. Kate had given her the towels last Thanksgiving. Ellie perched on the edge of the bed. She touched Kate's shoulder. "Why don't you wipe your face?"

"You wipe your face!" Kate screamed. It was a stupid reply. Kate knew that.

"What can I do to help?" Ellie asked politely.

"Tell me it's not true," Kate sobbed into the pillow.

"It *is* true." Ellie's monotone made Kate shiver. "I can't belong to you."

Kate couldn't breathe. She pounded the floor with her fists. She pulled off her leather tie and rolled it into a ball of black in the corner.

"Breathe," Ellie said in a voice from Mars. It was the voice that had arrived during the past week, since the betrayal. It was the voice of a guilty, worried friend, not a lover.

Kate pulled herself up and looked at herself in the bathroom mirror. Her face was pale and puffy.

"Will you stay tonight?" Ellie stood behind her.

"It hurts too much."

"What will you do?"

"I don't know."

"You shouldn't drive right now."

Kate laughed. "Why do you care?"

"Stay here. Take a nap. I'll be back at five, and we'll have dinner and watch a movie."

"You think I could sleep?" Kate found her bag and pulled a pair of her jeans from the drawer in the ex-husband's bureau. Then she opened another drawer and took her dildos. She felt ridiculous taking the dildos, but she didn't have enough clothes here to make her exit long and slow and painful.

Without saying good-bye she walked past Ellie, holding the wobbling dildos in her hands.

She sat at the steering wheel. Where was she going to go? She wanted to roar off, to hurt Ellie with a noisy, wordless exit. She turned on the ignition and reached for her sunglasses. She had left her sunglasses in the kitchen. She went back to the house. Ellie was smoking a cigarette on the deck.

"I left my sunglasses." Kate looked down at her hand. She had cut her knuckle banging on the bedroom floor.

"Let me fix your hand." Ellie's voice was tired and mechanical. She tried to pull Kate to the kitchen sink as she would have done to wash Nathan's hands after his oatmeal breakfast.

"Don't touch me." It was Kate's only power, to refuse to let Ellie wash her cut.

Kate spotted Ellie's cigarettes on the kitchen table. She pulled off the filter and lit one. The first drag made her dizzy; on the second puff she felt high. Ellie said nothing. She followed Kate into the living room and sat next to her on the couch where Nathan jumped each day.

"Why are you smoking?"

Kate dialed Stacey. "Because I'm an addict. That's what addicts do when they're in pain. They use. You should know that. You're using sex the same way."

Stacey's phone was ringing. "I am at Ellie's," Kate said. "It's over."

"What did she say?"

"She doesn't want to be lovers."

"Are you okay?"

"She's invited me to stay, but I don't think I can stand it."

"Come here, Katie," Stacey said gently.

"I think I need to go home."

"Don't go home," she said. "You shouldn't be alone."

"Tomorrow is my birthday," Kate said. "Ellie was going to take me out."

"I'll take you out. Come here. Please, Katie."

This must really be happening, Kate thought. "Ellie says I can stay here." Ellie patted her leg. Kate pulled it away.

"Does being with Ellie comfort you?"

"No," Kate whispered. "But I'm afraid to drive."

"Take the bus to San Francisco. I'll pick you up."

"I'm afraid I'll hit someone."

"Take the bus. You wouldn't want to kill someone else. You let them die of their own broken heart, okay?"

Kate pulled the filter off another Merit and lit it. It made her feel stoned. "Ellie wants me to take a nap while she goes to see Simon's psychiatrist. But Nathan and the baby-sitter will be here any minute."

"Please, come here." Stacey was using her voice for coaxing someone down off a tenth-story window ledge.

Kate inhaled. Ellie was not going to stop her.

In the kitchen Kate cut another cigarette and smoked it. For a moment she felt powerful.

"You look different," Ellie said.

"I am different," Kate said, enjoying her moment of confidence. "I know who you really are now. I know what you are capable of."

"If you stayed, we could go riding in the morning. Would you like that?"

Kate looked slowly around the room. *This is the last time,* she thought as she studied the bookcase, the leather album of Ellie's wedding pictures, the television where they had watched the endless videos, her Ping-Pong painting of the two of them, so happy on the night of their reunion.

"I'd like to buy you a birthday present."

Kate stared at her.

"Edward's has some beautiful white azaleas."

"You've given me your birthday present."

Ellie disappeared into the bedroom. She came out wearing a black sweater and gray skirt. "We're going to decide where Simon will live when he's released."

Kate did not reply. It would not affect her now. Where Simon lived was Alyson's concern.

They both got into their cars.

"Call me tonight," Ellie said.

Kate shook her head. "I won't call you."

Ellie looked at her, confused. "Why does it have to be this way? Why can't you call me?"

"Don't you know?"

Ellie's black car followed Kate's up to the highway entrance. Kate saw her in the rearview mirror following at a safe, cautious distance. Ellie stayed behind Kate all the way to Burlingame, where, at the exit, her black Rover turned up the off-ramp. *And that is that,* Kate thought. *It's over.*

Chapter **20**

In the morning Kate was sure she was dead. Driving to Point Reyes in Stacey's Rabbit soothed her; to be going someplace, anyplace with her best friend, helped her out of her brain, which was under siege, frazzled from lying all night on Stacey's futon, staring up at the ceiling, listening to cars go by on 24th Street, trying to figure out what had gone wrong. It was raining lightly now, and rain on her birthday, Kate decided, was an auspicious omen because of the drought.

"I still think," Stacey said as they headed through the green hills of the San Geronimo Valley, "that the ideal relationship is several relationships, so you never get too dependent and merged with any one."

Kate groaned.

"Think about it. Everyone knows that the others exist or may exist. That's part of the agreement. No names are named. Everyone is very discreet."

"It's hard enough having one lover."

"But it beats the 'till death do us part' dream that ends in tragedy," Stacey said.

Kate felt the knife. "Doesn't she miss me, Stace? Doesn't she wonder how I am?"

Stacey was wearing blue jeans and a navy sweater, a Mariners' baseball cap mashing down her curly blond Afro. She had the beginnings of a cold. "She's probably still enjoying her escape."

The words hurt. "She'll get bored."

"Not if she keeps finding new lovers so easily."

Kate felt sick. "But it happened so fast."

Stacey dug some chewing gum from her pocket and handed a stick to Kate. "That's how Ellie does things. She doesn't think; she acts. It's the surgical method. She offed her husband that quickly. Maybe it's more merciful."

"But if she loved me on Monday, I don't see how she could cut me off on Friday. That's inhuman."

They had passed the low clapboard storefronts of Inverness and were headed through the National Seashore, over the ridge toward Great Beach. "At least you can console yourself with the knowledge that her relationship with Alyson won't be like your relationship. You two were really close. Ellie's looking for escape now. This new one will unravel."

"When?" Kate asked eagerly. Tomorrow would not be soon enough.

"A month, three months, maybe a year."

Kate rubbed her eyes. "I can't take a year of this."

Stacey patted her knee. "But it will happen. They'll get closer, and Alyson will make demands, and Ellie will lose interest. Alyson's role is to divert her, not to be her partner."

Kate stared into the huge expanse of gray ocean in front of them. "What was *my* role?"

Stacey considered the question. "Your role was to get her out of her marriage."

"So I'm herstory," Kate finished.

A wind was blowing off the Pacific as waves crashed and smashed against the beach. A fine drizzle dampened the blue lupine and pampas grass in the dunes. They walked slowly, the water, the rhythm of waves, the salt air comforting Kate. "Alyson has money. That's why she likes her."

Stacey stuck her hands in her pockets. "She won't get any of Alyson's money. Maybe some little bonuses. Vacations. Gifts." Stacey cocked her head to one side. "But ultimately the sex question will come up with Alyson."

Kate glanced at two teenagers in Grateful Dead tie-dyed shirts wading in the surf and thought of Simon, scared and alone in the hospital. "If I were prettier...maybe that's it."

Stacey stopped and picked up a piece of brown kelp. "Is Alyson beautiful?"

"I don't know."

"It's not beauty." Stacey swung the seaweed around in a circle, forcing Kate to jump it.

"Well, sex appeal," Kate said breathlessly. "I wasn't sexy enough. I should have dressed in leather and lace, like those women in the porn films."

Stacey laughed and continued to swing the kelp. "Ellie's the one who's not sexy enough."

"Well, if I'd sold more paintings. Ouch!" The kelp rapped Kate's shins. Stacey dropped the seaweed on the sand.

"She's in awe of your work, Kate. That's why she liked you in the first place."

Kate blew air out of her cheeks. "Yeah, but if I'd had the money to share the rent on the big house, she'd have — "

Stacey groaned. "What kind of relationship is that, Katie? If you have to do all the accommodating?"

Kate was silent. Had she done all the accommodating? Yes, she'd gone to Ellie's on weekends, adjusted to Simon's moods and Nathan's constant, frantic presence. In recent months she had worked around Ellie's open houses and real estate schedules and Simon's hospitalization. Still, she had liked being part of Ellie's family life, of that normal, suburban, married lifestyle that she had never experienced. The world of babysitters and car pools and troubled teenagers had enriched her life and certainly her painting, which had thrived on the people and paradoxes and suburban scapes and twists of Ellie Webster and Turkey Run.

They walked on for another hour, seeing almost no one, studying the stones, comparing the pretty ones, searching for seals in the surf. Kate had not run in days, and her muscles were grateful for this long, slow stretch. She could almost breathe.

"I have a theory," Stacey began as they turned back at the cliffs for the car. "Ellie's trouble is her fear of being a lesbian."

"Really?" Maybe this would explain it all.

"She hates herself for wanting women, and she resents her women lovers because they remind her she's a lesbian and keep her from enjoying the privileges of married life. As long as she's sneaking around, having affairs instead of relationships, and as long as there's intrigue, she can feel good about herself because it's not a real, committed relationship. With you she had to admit she was a lesbian because she really loved you, and that was intolerable."

Kate studied a dead cormorant covered in oil, lying in the sand just above the tide line. "She always said she liked me because I was out as a lesbian."

"But she can't love you or any other woman until she can accept that it's okay for *her* to be out."

Kate inhaled a long breath of ocean air. "That could take years."

Stacey nodded, reaching for a thin razor shell, which she handed to Kate. "The thing you have to do is figure out why you stayed so long."

Kate swallowed. "I loved her. I'm in love with her."

Stacey tossed a pebble into the ocean. They watched it splash. "Ellie needs a satellite, not an equal partner. She sets it up that way."

"If I was her satellite" — Kate was starting to cry as her eyes followed the flight of five pelicans skimming above the breakers — "then why did *she* break it off? She was getting all the services."

Stacey said nothing. Kate tried to focus on the sound of the waves breaking, the tingle of the light rain on her cheeks, the pleasure of her best friend's company. "You are a child of the universe, deserving to love and be loved." That's what the nice lady on the self-hypnosis tape would say. But Kate felt like Hiroshima.

Stacey handed her the telephone. *Please let it be Ellie. Please let her be calling to say she's made a terrible mistake.* "It's Lucy Stone," Stacey whispered. "Ellie told her you were here."

"I'm a victim of the lesbian relationship wars," Kate said grimly to her agent.

"What?"

"Didn't Ellie tell you?"

"Tell me what?"

"We broke up Friday. She has a new lover."

"Katie, I'm sorry." There was a long pause. "Can we have lunch on Monday? I'm in San Francisco."

"I'm a wreck."

"Be a wreck."

"It's a deal." As Kate gave Lucy directions to her house, she saw that Stacey was relieved that Kate would have someone to hang with on Monday.

Kate heard footsteps, then the cowbell ringing on the front door. She crawled from her bed in her sweatpants and T-shirt and opened the door. Lucy Stone — in jeans and a red sweater — hugged her. It was strange to have Lucy Stone, whom she associated with New York, here in her little cottage in Sausalito.

Kate ground coffee beans. "I'm the only one of Ellie's problems she could get rid of. She's stuck with her crazy sons and her divorce and her real estate, so I'm the sacrificial lamb."

"What a fool."

"Thanks," Kate smiled.

Lucy hesitated. "I'm thinking of opening a gallery here."

"In San Francisco?"

"Maybe," Lucy said.

"Cool."

Kate drove Lucy to the Tennessee Valley, to her trail piercing through the hills to the ocean that always felt like home to Kate. They walked down the dirt fire road, past hills of wildflowers — blue lupine and orange poppies — growing among the high green grass. Kate felt as if she'd been up for a week, hit by a sledgehammer, head pounding, legs heavy, shoulders tight. But the sage-filled air, the familiar trail, the blue spread of ocean helped.

On the beach at the south end of the cove by the huge sandstone cliff, they sat down in the sun in a patch of dry sand. Staring up at some gulls circling above them, Kate took a deep breath and made herself say what she dreaded. "I thought maybe you'd be glad Ellie and I broke up."

Lucy's eyes widened. "Why?"

She could feel herself blushing, which made her blush harder. "I thought maybe you wanted to...you know..." She stopped. "To see Ellie again."

Lucy looked surprised.

Kate picked up a dry stick and flicked it toward the water. "Sort of pick up with where you left off in Maine that summer. Romantically speaking."

Lucy swallowed and clenched her jaw. "Ellie was madly in love with you, Katie. She was miserable with her family. I was her diversion till she could get home. You were all we talked about. Your work, your romance in high school."

Kate smiled miserably. "She left me then; she left me again. I don't learn very quickly." Ellie had always been very evasive about what had happened in Maine with Lucy Stone, and Kate, fearing the worst, hadn't pressed it.

They watched a man park his mountain bike in the rack by the beach and walk up the cliff behind them. Kate dug into the sand with her fingers. "I know you slept together," she said, taking a chance.

Lucy looked up. "Ellie told you that?"

Kate knew it must be bad if Lucy was not denying it, just pushing her hands deeper into her pockets and gazing uncomfortably at the waves. "Ellie and I were the only two lesbians on Mount Desert — at least we felt like it. Everyone up there is WASP and straight and married."

"So you did — " Kate forced herself. She could never trust Lucy if she didn't know the truth. "Sleep together?"

Lucy coughed. "Kate, I'm sorry. You don't know how sorry."

Feeling the tears, Kate covered her face in her hands.

Lucy's touch on her shoulder made her feel more miserable. Ellie, even at the very start of their relationship, had made love with Lucy and lied about it.

"Katie?" Lucy squeezed her shoulder again. "If it's any consolation, we weren't in love. She was in love with you."

"Was she?" Kate wanted to believe Lucy.

Lucy picked up an oblong-shaped purple mussel shell. "She adored you. And I know it sounds strange, but I was much more interested in you as well. I'd seen your work for years. We talked nonstop about *you*."

Kate pressed her heels into the sand. "Then why did you...?"

"She was very..." Lucy paused. "Seductive."

Kate inhaled. "She said nothing happened."

"It *was* nothing, really."

"I know you had no loyalty to me. I understand that. It was Ellie who — "

Lucy moved closer. "You don't know how I wish I could tell you it wasn't true."

Kate felt sincerity in Lucy's voice, but Ellie had seemed sincere too. "Are you going to see her on this trip?"

Lucy looked hard at Kate. "I don't even like Ellie Webster. It may be hard for you to believe because you love her so much, but I think she's a manipulative, self-centered woman. I thought that before she broke up with you, and I feel it even more so now. I wouldn't care if I never saw Ellie again in my life."

Kate stood up slowly and walked down to the water, tiptoe-ing barefoot into the icy waves. She stood, hypnotized by the blue, by the sound, by the cry of the gulls, by the sight miles out of a white sail leaning against the ocean. *Ellie and Lucy were lovers.*

They ate Mexican food on the dock in Tiburon. Kate man-aged a bowl of *sopa de tortilla.*

"Would you like to fly to L.A. with me tomorrow?"

"Thanks." Kate leaned on her elbows. "I'd just be avoiding the inevitable."

"Which is?" Lucy looked at her curiously.

"Starting my life again. Getting used to the fact that Ellie is gone. For the past year and a half, it's been a partnership. Now it's just me. Everything feels so strange. It's like she's dead."

Lucy looked down at the check and paid the bill. "This isn't a seduction. I have two beds. It's a huge room."

Kate blushed. What difference did it make if she put off cleaning the studio and trying to work? She'd be unhappy whatever she did, so why not hang out with Lucy? She could clean the studio tomorrow. "What hotel?"

"The Stanford Court." Lucy smiled. "They've got TV in the bathroom."

Kate laughed.

"Then it's a deal?"

"But I'm not going to L.A."

They drove to Russian Hill in two cars. Lucy ordered room service for dinner, and they watched the Olympic ice-skating finals from the enormous king-size bed. Kate took a long hot bath while Lucy made phone calls.

The presence of another person helped the sad, panicky feeling and the unbearable longing for Ellie. She wanted to call Ellie, to pick up the phone and say, "Hey, it's me. What's up?" But Stacey had begged her to hold off as long as she could. Until something changed with Ellie and Alyson, she said, talking with Ellie would only hurt more.

Kate felt shy when she came out of her bath, like a child spending the night away from home for the first time. But the sound of the TV, the whirring of the heating system, Lucy's gentle Southern accent telling Kate stories about friends in New York and L.A., lulled her to sleep.

When she woke at 2 A.M., the peace of mind she'd felt at bedtime had dissolved. All she felt was pain, then anger. Ellie and Lucy Stone had been lovers.

How could they?

They could because Ellie seduced her and Lucy, who had no loyalty to me at the time, fell for it. Kate stared into the dark, heard sirens outside on California Street. What was she doing here with Lucy Stone? Lucy had been Ellie's lover. In the darkness she found her clothes and left the hotel, driving home alone to Sausalito.

Chapter 21

Being alone by herself was like living with a killer. Every morning at 5 A.M. Kate crawled from bed, made coffee, walked to the ocean in the dark, then drove to a 7 A.M. AA meeting at the log cabin in Mill Valley. Eddy, the bank robber who had spent thirty-four years in prison, always said, "I love you, Kate" and told her to keep coming back.

After the meeting she started running along the bike path with a young woman named Rayanne, who was short and pretty, with blond hair pulled back in a ponytail. She spoke with a flat Midwestern accent. "I binged last night," Rayanne told Kate one morning as they passed a heron perched on one leg in the marsh, scanning the still water for food. "I had three quarts of Häagen-Dazs and purged."

"You what?"

"Threw up."

Kate watched the heron spear a tiny fish.

"I'm bulimic," Rayanne said, flicking back her ponytail. "I'm powerless over ice cream, and my life has become unmanageable."

"I'm powerless over Ellie, and my life has become unmanageable."

Kate spoke to Stacey every day. Sometimes she spent the weekend at Stacey's.

"I have news for you," Stacey said, three months after the breakup.

"Of Ellie?" Kate's heart fibrillated.

"Do you want to hear? It's from Mary Jane." Mary Jane was Stacey's lesbian doctor friend who lived in Turkey Run.

"Will it upset me?"

"Ellie and Alyson had a fight. Alyson told Ellie she was ruining her life for an eighteen-year-old boy."

"Is Simon living at home now?" Kate asked.

"Yes. And he's driving Alyson crazy."

"Good." While it was extremely satisfying to hear that Ellie and Alyson were fighting over Simon, the reminder that Ellie was so deeply involved with Alyson was painful.

"Want to hear more?" Stacey asked.

"I don't know."

"Ellie told Mary Jane that Simon misses you and wonders where you are."

"Why doesn't he call me if he misses me?"

Stacey inhaled. "He's taking his cues from his mother. His loyalty is to her."

This news of Ellie deepened the black hole in her chest. She wanted to call Ellie so much, her whole body ached. "Nothing I can do will get her back, right?"

"Not now. Not yet."

"Can't I call her?" Kate begged hopelessly.

"Not if she's still seeing Alyson. You'll just feel worse. She has nothing new to tell you."

Kate did not pick up the phone.

She couldn't paint because painting was too solitary. Doing massage, touching strangers at the spa, helped. It kept her from crying.

"Mary Jane met Alyson," Stacey said one morning.

"Oh, God." Kate sat down on the couch.

"She said Alyson was dark and strange and had a limp handshake."

"But she's blond. How could she be dark?"

"She has a dark presence."

"Did Mary Jane hate her?"

"Mary Jane says she's sleazy and boring and alcoholic. And Ellie is all strange and flirty and sexy around her."

Kate's heart stopped. Ellie was sexy around Alyson. Kate felt she'd been whacked with a hammer. Clearly Ellie didn't miss her, not even a little. Ellie had made a painless transition into her new life with Alyson. "Don't tell me any more," Kate said cautiously.

"There isn't any more," Stacey said.

A lesbian named Marcia, knowing of Kate's sadness, invited her to attend a Lakota Indian sweat in Palo Alto.

"What if I become psychotic?" Kate was only half kidding.

"Have you ever been psychotic?"

"No."

"Then you won't get psychotic. The sweat may help you feel better."

Marcia was an Episcopalian minister, a witch, a part-time Buddhist, a student of Native American ceremonies, and a psychotherapist. Her pale brown hair, sad eyes, and glitter-specked glasses made her look like a housewife from the '50s. She was thirty-five and spoke with the stiff, careful enunciation of a schoolteacher. "You didn't eat anything, did you?" Marcia asked when she picked Kate up by the freeway in Sausalito.

"Nothing," Kate said.

"No coffee?"

"Nothing. I promise."

"Good. We try to purify ourselves before a sweat."

Marcia drove like a wild woman down Highway 280 to Palo Alto. She wouldn't take Highway 101, even though Kate begged her to, explaining that 280 could drive her off the deep end because it reminded her of Ellie. Marcia wobbled and braked and switched lanes at high speeds, all the while telling Kate about her Lakota Indian spirituality classes with Eagle Bear, the medicine man. Kate gripped the dashboard and pressed her feet into the floor; despite her morbidity she did not want to die in a car crash with Marcia.

The trip south took them on the same route Kate had traveled on Black Friday, the day of her execution by Ellie. Past Crystal Springs Reservoir, past the turnoff for Half Moon Bay, past the horse barns near Turkey Run.

"I think I see Ellie," Kate told Marcia. "In the black car ahead."

Marcia was cool and matter-of-fact. "Try not to think about her."

Kate tried not to, but her stomach buckled when she saw the black Rover ahead in which she was sure she could make out Ellie driving Nathan and Alyson. But as they passed she saw only a man with a Doberman pinscher and a baby in the backseat.

"I hope this sweat will help me," Kate said as her breathing returned to normal.

"It can take several days to feel the changes."

Kate wanted relief immediately. She had brought the Mayan fertility goddess from her altar.

They parked at a low one-level ranch house in Palo Alto, where middle-aged members of the Woodstock Nation were gathering in beaded headbands, brightly colored Guatemalan shirts, embroidered jeans and jackets, and moccasins. Kate noted with envy that some were drinking coffee.

Marcia led Kate outside into the unruly, gigantic, overgrown backyard where several little girls were throwing water bombs at each other. An African-American man in beautiful beads and dreadlocks banged on a conga drum. Beyond the swimming pool, which was covered in turquoise plastic, and behind a high green hedge, Kate spied a tiny round hut covered in blankets and black garbage bags.

"That's the sweat lodge," Marcia said.

It was hard for Kate to believe that a miracle of healing was going to take place in the funky plastic shack. Near the lodge some men in blue jeans and flip-flops were building a fire, tossing on logs from a huge woodpile.

"It takes a cord of wood to get the rocks hot enough," Marcia explained. A few steps from the fire, some women were huddled on a huge tarpaulin of blue plastic, making something.

"Prayer necklaces," Marcia whispered. She picked up a small square of red fabric. "Each little red cloth contains your prayer. You put tobacco in and tie it up with a string."

A woman, Sondra, showed Kate what to do. Most of the hippie women had the soft, well-fed look of mothers. "Each red square," Sondra said, holding up a tiny red cloth, "represents a prayer you want the Great Spirit to answer. After the sweat you throw your necklace into the fire, and your prayers will be answered."

Kate understood. "It's like letters to Santa Claus on Christmas Eve. You throw them on the fire so Santa can read the smoke and give you the presents you want."

"It's pretty much like that," Sondra smiled.

A lanky cowboy in a Stetson and tooled boots approached. His black hair was pulled into a ponytail, and he wore a snap-down Western shirt and skintight Levi's and had dark leathery skin.

"Eagle Bear," Marcia said breathlessly. "This is my friend Kate."

Eagle Bear grinned, switching his coffee mug to his cigarette hand to shake Kate's hand. "This your first sweat?"

"First time." Kate smiled from the tarpaulin.

"You're not on your moon, are you?"

Kate glanced at Marcia.

"Your period," her friend said quickly. "You're not menstruating?"

"No," Kate said uncertainly.

"Good." Eagle Bear nodded. "Have you made your prayers?"

181

"Not yet," Kate said. But Kate knew what they would be. She would ask for Ellie to come back.

"The Great Spirit answers all of our prayers," Eagle Bear said, taking a long drag on his Camel. "But not necessarily in the time and the way we want him to."

"They say that in AA too," Kate said.

Eagle Bear stared at Kate.

"Alcoholics Anonymous," Marcia said helpfully.

Eagle Bear laughed. "Maybe I should go to AA. We sure drank too much wine last night. I need more coffee." He strolled toward the house.

"He likes you," Marcia whispered.

"Really?" Kate was pleased, despite her surprise.

"Tobacco's sacred to Native Americans," Marcia said, taking some tiny leaves from the leather pouch around her neck while Kate watched the fire makers place peace pipes on the altar by the sweat lodge.

"Don't use so much tobacco," Marcia whispered.

More people joined them on the tarpaulin and made their necklaces. Marcia felt it her duty to educate Kate. "It's not always good to pray for specific outcomes. Sometimes it's best to pray that the will of the Great Spirit be done."

But Kate had decided. She had made seven prayers asking for Ellie back. Their new life wouldn't be easy, not in the beginning. They'd have a lot to discuss, a lot of what Rayanne in AA called "trust issues," but once they got through the initial stuff, they'd rebuild, maybe move to Mexico as they'd always planned.

Twenty-five half-naked celebrants bowed at the altar before crawling into the lodge. Kate's heart thudded nervously. She wanted the scar in her heart to be gone when this sweat was over. She entered just before Eagle Bear, who sat next to her chanting, while the men from outside shoveled orange, hot, glowing rocks into the fireplace in the middle of the tent. Eagle Bear closed the flap of the sweat lodge.

"The stones will talk to you if you listen. Sometimes you

will see faces and pictures in the stones. Watch. Listen. Pray."
As Eagle Bear chanted in Lakota, Kate stared at the stones,
waiting for a hallucination. Eagle Bear's girlfriend, Sondra,
beat on a drum. *Boom, boom, boom, boom.*

Kate was starting to get warm. Eagle Bear signaled a fire
man to bring more hot rocks to the fire. The drumming continued, and the chanting and the heat increased as the stones
glowed bright orange in the dark. *Boom, boom, boom, boom,
boom.* Kate's face was exploding.

Eagle Bear lit the peace pipe and then passed it to his left.
Everyone inhaled a long, deep drag of the sacred tobacco. The
smoke made Kate dizzy. She had not smoked tobacco since
her execution in Ellie's kitchen. She was starting to spin.
When would they open the flap? A woman who had been sobbing, quietly rose and left the lodge. Kate wanted to leave too.
But she didn't want to be cowardly. She would try to tough it
out, despite the claustrophobic heat.

"You're doing very well," Eagle Bear whispered.

Kate was flattered. She could not leave the lodge now, after
the medicine man had complimented her. She did not want
him to think she was a wimp, although her lungs were beginning to melt. She wondered how much heat it would take for
her to actually go up in flames. Leaning back, she tried to get
down and away where it was cooler, close to the floor. Sweat
poured from her forehead and breasts and between her legs.
Her tank top and underpants were drenched. The dirt on the
floor was turning to mud from all the sweating.

She sat up again. *Wham* — a blast of heat in the face. The
fire men were placing more hot rocks on the fire. She braced
herself. *Boom, boom, boom* went the drum. They were chanting again to the stone spirits.

Layers and layers of sweat dripped from Kate's insides. *I
am in the inferno,* she thought. *Please, help me. Help me,
someone.* She could not swallow. Every blood vessel in her
skull was pounding. She remembered she had not eaten since
yesterday. *Help me,* she called to the Great Spirit. *Release me*

from this heat.

She stared at the rocks, looked away, then back again. A face. Yes, she saw a face. Eyes, a forehead, a chin. She might melt to death in this sweat lodge, but she could see a face now in the rocks. She squinted. Who was it? *Help!* she called again. Who was it? It was Lucy Stone. *Lucy Stone.* What was Lucy doing here?

Everyone was chanting. A woman in the back was sobbing. *Release me,* Kate asked the rock face of Lucy. *Help me, Lucy. Do something. Quickly.*

Eagle Bear shouted something mystical and snatched open the flap of the lodge. Cold air rushed into the tent. They were leaving now one by one, thanking the stone spirits, the Great Spirit for answering their prayers, walking in a clockwise direction. Kate was the first to go.

The grass was emerald; the sky, a pale blue. The air had the taste of spring. Everyone was smeared with mud. Kate stood by the huge fire, staring down at her dirty legs, feeling like a mud man of the Asahi River, like a wild thing. She had never, ever sweat so much.

Kate saw Marcia standing alone by the fire, pale and withdrawn. Staring into the flames, Kate pulled off her prayer necklace, studied the seven red wet squares of tobacco, and tossed them into the fire. She heard the necklace hiss in the flames and watched it crinkle and disappear in the heat. *That's it,* Kate thought. *She's coming back.*

People wandered the yard in a trance as Kate washed herself with a garden hose in the back near the lodge. Mud swirled off her feet and legs and arms. She dried herself with a towel, found her clothes in her knapsack, put them on in the bushes. It was wonderful to be dry and clean, a baby wrapped in swaddling clothes. For the first time in months, Kate felt cheerful.

In the kitchen the Woodstock Nation was warming the food for the potluck. Kate steamed the broccoli she had brought. There was homemade bread, chili, guacamole, vegetables, salad of every kind, rice, black beans, hummus, and baba ganouj.

"You did well," Eagle Bear said to Kate as she drained her broccoli.

Kate felt wonderful — light and free and very hungry.

"Did you see anything in the stones?" asked Eagle Bear.

"I think I saw my friend Lucy from New York."

He nodded sagely. "Whoever appears in the stones is important. Maybe a guide."

Slowly, on sweat time, the food was placed on a long table in the living room. There were dips and grains and breads and steamed vegetables and pots full of the best food Kate had ever tasted. She sat on the big couch between Eagle Bear and Sondra. Drums were thudding outside. The people seemed different now, no longer hippies pretending to be Native Americans but regular people eating and talking and celebrating together. Kate realized suddenly that for the first time since February, she was not thinking about Ellie. Was that the secret of the sweat? You can't be in that cauldron of heat and think about anything except being cool again. Sweating go is letting go.

Someone strummed an acoustic guitar. The notes were soft, like flannel blankets, and the voices were sweet and soothing. Kate did not feel separate and self-absorbed and anxious. She was in love with the chili beans and guacamole and homemade bread and tofu casserole. She felt, she realized, like a human being.

When the light faded, people began to pack up their pots and towels and muddy underclothes. Everyone was hugging. Kate hugged too.

Driving back in the dark, Marcia did not speed maniacally as before. When Kate saw the sign for Turkey Run Road, she felt a sudden pain. *If I let her,* Kate thought, *she'll inhabit me again.* She called silently to the warm spirit, the Lucy Stone rock she'd seen in the sweat. *Help!* When Marcia began to talk and tell her about Eagle Bear and the Lakota ways and the fear

185

she'd felt in the sweat, Kate could listen, could hear, feeling only a small part of herself detach from the car and hurry up Turkey Run Road to tell Ellie she loved her. More than ever.

□ Part IV □

Chapter 22

When Nathan's school bus honked, Ellie held her son's soft, small hand in hers and walked with him out the kitchen door, around the side of the house, past the stalls to the parking area by the corral. She waved to the driver and watched Nathan scramble up the steps, her heart tugging at the sight of little Jennifer, with her thick blue glasses, strapped to her electronic chair, barely able to move. "Good morning, Mrs. Webster," she said cheerfully.

"That's a very pretty dress you're wearing, Jennifer."

"Thank you, Mrs. Webster," she replied so sweetly that Ellie turned away to hide her tears.

So unfair, she thought, opening the barn door. She switched on the light, pulled a bale of hay from the last stall, and dumped it in the paddock. *Damn.* Simon had not shoveled the manure.

In the kitchen Ellie made another cup of coffee and tried to read the *Chronicle* headlines. Words and places — Iran, Sarajevo, Beijing — bounced meaninglessly through her brain. Last night's conversation with Kate had disturbed her more than she'd realized, had made her raw and irritable. She should have been nicer when Alyson offered to take her to Puerto Vallarta for ten days. And she should not have said to Simon what she did.

Ellie stared down at the coffee mug, GREETINGS FROM SAUSALITO, that Kate had given her soon after they'd met. For months now she'd wanted to call Kate, invite her down for a ride, talk with her as a friend instead of waiting to hear secondhand news of her through Mary Jane via Stacey. Kate had made it so difficult for Ellie, asking her never to call, refusing contact of any kind. Ellie had respected that, but when she heard from Mary Jane that Kate was painting again, was not so angry and bitter, she succumbed to her urge to call. Last night, when Alyson was in bed and Simon was studying in his room, she'd phoned.

Ellie flicked open the gold monogrammed lighter from Alyson and lit a cigarette. The conversation with Kate had not been what she had expected — or wanted. Kate had sounded distant and removed, said Ellie had a wall she put up to keep from getting close, then insisted Ellie explain why she had slept with Lucy Stone that summer they'd met. She'd been caught off guard, had no defense except to say she was still drinking then and thought somehow sleeping with Lucy would help Kate get a show in New York. Was that true? Or had Ellie done it because the opportunity was there and she felt turned on and Kate was 3,000 miles away?

She put out her cigarette and carried Nathan's laundry into his little room off the kitchen, folding his underpants and T-shirts carefully into his dresser drawers. Beneath the scent of baby powder, there was still the lingering smell of leather bridles and saddles from all the years this had been the tack room. *Of course, I have a wall. Everyone has walls. You can't go around spending every moment of your life feeling things. That's a luxury only artists or heiresses like Alyson can afford.*

"Take some deep breaths," that psychotherapist Alyson had paid for kept repeating. Ellie had lain naked in front of her, feeling fat and embarrassed, trying to breathe through her belly, trying to experience her feelings. "Breathe, Ellie. Breathe," the woman, Joyce, kept intoning in her singsong voice. "Let yourself feel." But why should she? Why should she focus on her longing for Kate or the rage she felt at Simon or her sorrow at Nathan's tragic disability?

Ellie looked at the clock. Was it already 9:15? She must start making her cold calls, then send brochures to whomever she reached. Then she'd go to the office meeting, give her manager a progress report, and ring doorbells, introducing herself to the residents of her target neighborhood. That's what her manager advised, although Ellie hated all that selling, all that asking favors from strangers.

Kate and Lucy are involved, Ellie decided suddenly, annoyed that no one had told her Lucy was opening a gallery in San Francisco. The image of Kate and Lucy together, of Lucy sitting on the couch in Kate's little cottage above the water troubled Ellie, who reached for the leftover pizza Alyson had brought home last night. There was a plastic tub of spaghetti in the back and next to it an open bottle of chardonnay — another of Alyson's provisions. Ellie frowned. She'd stopped drinking when she'd met Kate but had started again with Alyson, just a drink every now and then to prove to herself she was not an alcoholic.

"She's using you, Alyson," Simon had said at breakfast this morning. "She'll use you and dump you just like she dumped Kate. Can't you see that?"

"Goddamn it!" Ellie had roared. "Shut your mouth."

"Fuck you!" Simon had yelled, slamming out the door.

"You worthless piece of shit!" Ellie had screamed. "I wish you'd die!"

That was cruel, Ellie thought, swallowing the last of the pizza. Her rage would only make Simon feel worse and make her feel more guilty. What if some day she were made to pay for her anger, for her seductions, for her ability to cut people out of her life without a second thought? She tossed the cardboard pizza box into the garbage and stood up. *Get hold of yourself. Quash this panic.*

The buzzer on the dryer startled her. *Do something. Move.* Outside and along the stalls she walked, depositing a new load of bedsheets and towels into the washer, stopping in front of the paddock to look at the cut on Isis' left hind leg. Now that was an accomplishment, wasn't it? To own four horses and ride every day? Nina would have approved of that, even if the horses were unschooled trail mounts, not hunter-jumpers.

Simon's wrong about Kate. I didn't use her, Ellie thought, looking across the road to the Farbs' yellow barn and ring and down in the distance toward San Francisco Bay. She wanted to keep this place forever, for the boys, for herself. It was the home where her future had seemed bright and fun and promising. Now she was living in a horse barn, charging her lesbian lover a fee to ride, raising one son who was mentally ill, another no smarter than a dog.

Simon would get better. Of course he would. And she'd apologize to Simon this afternoon as soon as he came in. Yes, he'd been rude, but her words had been a little hard, and he was still vulnerable, Dr. Veda said, despite being sober for nearly six months.

Life wasn't easy for her either. She was learning to control herself, forcing herself to work, but — the latest letter from Nicky's lawyer in the mail basket above the kitchen table caught her eye. Nicky had escaped all this. He was living on easy street with Danielle — no kids, no responsibilities, getting checks from his mother, taking Simon or Nathan when it pleased him. The divorce had barely touched his life; hers had come crashing down.

Pulling the clean sheet across the mattress on which she and Nicky had lain on for seventeen years, the bed that dipped on the side where she had slept as far away from Nicky as possible, she glanced at the new bedside photograph of Nathan with Theresa, his young Thai teacher. What a saint she was — devoted and selfless as she worked with those innocent, tragic children! Perhaps she would invite Theresa riding, get some advice from her about Nathan, who was becoming more moody and harder to control. What if — Ellie found her legs softening, her heart racing slightly at the thought — she were to touch Theresa's slender waist, feel those beautiful, perfectly shaped breasts, that flawless, smooth Oriental skin.

You are sick. She finished making the bed with a vengeance. *You are the decadent city of Venice falling into the sea. Imagine seducing a young girl half your age, your own son's teacher.* She pulled the blue eiderdown over the bed. Nicky had given her that quilt on her birthday, the day before he had carelessly pushed Simon's stroller into an oncoming car on 81st Street. He had been admiring the cornice work on a Louis Sullivan Fifth Avenue brownstone when a cab pulled in front of them. The doctors said he'd recovered completely, but was that the real beginning of Simon's illness, whatever his illness was?

Ellie found her briefcase and opened her datebook. She must stop this brooding. She must get to work, make some calls, take charge of her professional life.

"Are you going to see Kate again?" Alyson had asked her this morning. The question had infuriated Ellie. It was none of Alyson's business. If Alyson wanted exclusivity, monogamy, commitment, she should look elsewhere, not to her, Ellie had told her.

Alyson had broken into tears, which had been disconcerting.

"Kate doesn't want to see me," Ellie said more gently.

"Does that bother you?"

"What is this? An interrogation?" Why did this keep happening to Ellie? A sexy affair became something more, where people wanted answers, expected things. Perhaps she would have just one more bite of something before she made her calls. Studying the refrigerator, she was irritated by Alyson's bottle of chardonnay taking up so much room. She uncorked it and began to pour it down the drain. But the smell, the familiar oaky flavor of good white California wine, intrigued her. Finding one of the tulip-shaped glasses Kate had given her for her birthday, she filled it with wine. She could have the occasional drink without falling into the gutter. And today was a special day, a red-letter real estate day. She would be forceful, strong, upbeat. "*Salute!*" she said aloud, lifting the glass to her lips. She swallowed, took another sip, and frowned. *A little flat but not bad.*

Her lips on the crystal rim of the glass reminded her suddenly of Kate, of how nice it would be when Kate felt a little better to have her down for the day or to go up to Sausalito, above the water and the palm tree island, and hold that long, hard body in her arms again. It was just a matter of time before Kate would be ready. She could feel Kate's eyes on her breasts, her hands closing around her waist, feel Kate's legs, strong from running, press between hers. She slipped her hand into her panties, feeling her wetness from last night, from talking to Kate for almost an hour. What would be the harm of —

Ellie sat up, startled. A funny scraping was coming from the barn. Was it that raccoon again, the one that opened the oat bin by standing on the stool? Well — she glanced at her printout. She must get back to work. But this soft purring in her pelvis was disconcerting. Was it the wine? She turned back to the kitchen and saw the bottle of chardonnay. Of course, the wine. She had not felt that comforting, oozy glow in a long time.

She poured another glass, kissed the crystal lip, wondering why Kate had made it all so final. Ellie had not intended to stop seeing her completely, only to take the pressure off, break the boring sameness of monogamy. Was that so wrong? And Alyson had been so easy and light and fun, the perfect antidote to Kate's sobriety.

Just for fun, Ellie would have another glass of wine before her calls. She deserved a little reward after the past twenty-four hours — the upsetting phone call, the fight with Simon, the harsh words with Alyson. There wasn't much left; she'd finish the bottle and throw it away.

Ellie was pleased at how much better she felt. She'd make at least twenty calls, then go to the office meeting and tell her manager what she'd accomplished. Some agents — they were mostly all women — seemed quite fond of Ellie, like Willa, the sexy German with the Lebanese boyfriend. Willa had flirted with her one night at Le Pub, when Ellie hinted that if she liked women, Ellie would be a candidate. She must stop these fantasies. Work was the thing.

Opening her printout on the couch, Ellie picked up the receiver and dialed. An answering machine. *Not bad. A start.* She left her name and phone number in a voice she hoped was charming and professional. It had worked well enough on women over the years, all the times when Nicky had been away on business and she had flipped through her address book, picked up the phone, *et voilà,* a date. She made a little note on her sheet as her manager had told her to do, stating the date and time and outcome of her call. *Easy,* she thought. *Amazingly easy.* She made nine more calls, reached three answering machines, one housekeeper, two hang-ups, and three maybes.

Hadn't that work friend of Alyson's brought over a bottle of cabernet last week? Another little hit, she thought, opening the bottle, would assure an even more productive morning. One great day of calls was what she needed to get into the groove again, to show herself and her manager that she could farm for new prospects as well as any of the top sellers.

Now music. She switched on the amplifier and found the Bach Cantata No. 78 that Kate had adored because of the blissful duet between the two women, the most glorious love song in classical music, and pressed it into the CD player Alyson had given her. It felt good to be alive. Was it the wine? Was it talking to Kate last night? The awkward conversation was a first step. Anything could happen between two people who had loved as passionately as she and Kate, whose connection went back so far, it would never be extinguished by a painful misunderstanding. At Kate's cottage, surrounded by those paintings, by Kate's visions, under the green quilt, the windows open, the water below, they would swim again in the waves of their love.

Ellie stretched out her legs as the Bach whirled and spun a kaleidoscope of images around her — snorkeling in Mexico, rides up through the woods, sitting for her portrait, Kate's gaze penetrating her soul.

Work. Get to work. Ellie rose and looked into Simon's room, at the chaos of clothes draped over the bunk beds, piled on the floor, stuffed into the chair. Would he ever get it together? Would he ever have a job?

There it was again, that funny, odd, bumping noise. She would turn the music off, find the sound's source, then go to work, with a plan now — a handle on her day. Tonight, perhaps, as her reward for ringing doorbells, she'd write to Kate. Nothing heavy, nothing too serious, just a note to say what she'd been afraid to tell her last night on the phone with Alyson right there and Simon about to walk in the kitchen door. That she still loved her, still wanted her. She had not known that before, in the heat of passion last February, when Alyson had seduced her in that leather-seated Mercedes, taken her to Maui, teased her with the promise of buying Nicky's share of the house.

Ellie dumped the rest of the cabernet noir in the sink and closed the kitchen door behind her. The sun was hot but a pleasant kind of heat, not oppressive but a little dizzying. *Damn!* Alyson had left the hose unwound when she'd watered the horses this morning. *Maddening, her carelessness.*

She tossed her briefcase into the front seat, backing the car away from the barn, then stopped. Why was the barn door open? Had she forgotten to close it after removing the last load of laundry from the dryer? Is that how the raccoon had gotten in? Ellie shifted into neutral, left the car idling, and stared into the darkness. *I'm slightly drunk.*

She held on to the door, then heard it again, that scratching noise, then something else — a low raspy sound. She reached for the light switch. When her eyes adjusted to the darkness, she saw something, then looked away, then looked back. Simon's red high-tops poked out of the far stall, the empty one next to the saddle racks.

Ellie's heart spun. "Simon?" Stepping forward, she moved her eyes from his legs to his chest to his face. She inhaled quickly. *Nothing's wrong. He's fallen asleep, that's all.* "Simon?" she said again. "Why aren't you in school? Are you—" Ellie stooped over; his face was dead white. "Sweetheart?" She knelt next to her son, lifting him by the shoulders. His eyes did not open; his body was inert.

Call someone. A doctor. Call Henry Farb. He's at work. An ambulance? How long will that take? She flung open the barn doors, backing the Rover into the barn. Using all her strength, she pulled, then hoisted Simon's long body into the back of the car. Wet covered his jeans, and she saw now that saliva leaked from his open mouth. *Has he been drinking? Using drugs?*

Down the hill, past the horses, past the barns and paddocks and oak groves Ellie roared, trying to think where there was a hospital. That place next to the video store in Menlo Park was a hospital, wasn't it? She'd taken Simon to an AA meeting there. She tore through the stop sign by Edward's Store, passed the freeway entrance and the high school, ran three lights on Turkey Run Road. When she looked back at Simon, she heard her mother's voice. *Look what you've done to your son. Look where your selfishness has gotten you.*

"Simon, Simon, Simon," Ellie chanted. "I love you. I really do. I love you, I love you. You're going to be okay." She saw the high-rise building up ahead, on the right, and followed the neon signs to the emergency room. Car idling, she ran past a Hispanic woman in pink shorts carrying a crying baby.

"My son's in the car," she yelled to the receptionist.

"May I see your — "

"He's unconscious. Please. Help me!" The woman was moving too slowly. "Fuck!" Ellie said, running through the hall. She opened the back of the Land Rover and hauled Simon over her shoulder as two men in green wheeled a gurney toward her. They guided him onto the narrow bed. The smell of the hospital — baked chicken and rubber and alcohol — fought with the wine swirling in her stomach; she wanted to vomit. *Live, Simon, live!* she prayed as she followed the men and the gurney past the receptionist into a medical area filled with machines and curtained cubicles.

An angular bearded man of about forty with a kind face and wearing wire-rimmed glasses and green pajamas placed an oxygen mask over Simon's face while a nurse took his blood pressure and stuck a needle in his arm. "I'm Dr. Karnes," the man said, shining a flashlight into Simon's unmoving eyes. "When did you last see your son conscious?"

"He's unconscious?"

"I need information," the man said, loosening Simon's belt and pressing gently on his stomach.

Ellie chewed her thumbnail. "He was fine this morning."

"What time was that?"

What time is it now? The fucking wine. "He left around eight this morning. I found him this way about…a few minutes ago."

The man glanced at his watch. "Was he depressed? Anything troubling him?"

Why was he asking such questions? *Just save my son, Doctor. Don't let him die.* "Everything was troubling him. The divorce, school, Alyson, Kate, an exam this morning…" Ellie stopped. They were trying to stick a rubber tube down Simon's throat.

"He's gagging," said the doctor as the nurse forced Si's mouth open with her hands. "That's good. He still has the reflex. Do you have any idea what he ingested?"

"Ingested?"

"Do you keep any drugs at home? Valium? Aspirin? Any painkillers? Anything he might have taken? Has he been drinking?"

A small patch of dry skin on the doctor's cheek distracted her. "He's been clean and sober for almost six months."

He looked at her oddly. "What about tranquilizers? Antidepressants? Pain pills?"

She tried to think. Alyson kept a bottle of Tylenol in the medicine cabinet for her headaches, which Ellie had told her would go away by themselves if she stopped drinking. "Tylenol," Ellie said finally.

The doctor scribbled something on his clipboard and looked at Ellie. "How many were in the bottle?"

"I don't know. They're my lov — " Ellie stopped. "They belong to a friend."

He straightened and looked at Ellie with sympathetic brown eyes. "Mrs. Webster, I'm going to ask you to go back to the waiting room. Now that he's intubated, we'll wash out your son's stomach with activated charcoal, which will absorb whatever he's ingested. We'll know more about that in about an hour, when we see his blood work."

The doctor's calm professional voice comforted Ellie as she sat down outside next to a tall black youth holding a bloody towel over his eye.

They moved Simon upstairs to intensive care. Ellie drank coffee from a little pot they had for the families.

When Nicky arrived she was glad. His wavy brown hair seemed grayer than it had been a few weeks ago, when she'd seen him last. She didn't know what Nicky did in his office anymore now that he'd sold the crystal mine — for far less than they'd hoped — but he'd been there when she called.

He sat next to her in the orange chrome chair. "How is he?"

She found the piece of paper on which she'd written what the doctor said. "They stuck a tube into his stomach and washed him with activated charcoal, and they've given him something called Mucomyst to fight the effects of about thirty Extra Strength Tylenol, which is about eleven grams of acetaminophen, which is not good. He's on a respirator and getting IV fluids."

"Shit." Nicky rubbed his eyes. "What happened?"

Ellie was ashamed. "I was going to work around noon, and I found the barn door open. Si was lying in Isis' old stall, you know, the closest to the house." Her voice cracked as the tears came. "I put him in the car and brought him here."

"Good work." Nicky patted her arm.

Ellie fished a cigarette from her purse and lit it, hands trembling. "We had a terrible fight this morning. He was extremely rude, and I told him I wished he were dead." Ellie stared into Nicky's familiar brown eyes.

"I thought you weren't drinking."

"I'm not." Ellie covered her mouth with her hand.

He squinted at her.

"I had one glass of wine at lunch." She tried to make him understand. "He was terribly rude to both of us. I cannot have him behaving this way."

"Of course not."

"He tests me and tests me, Nickers."

"I know," Nicky said softly. "He's the same with us. Danielle says he's terribly unhappy."

Ellie bristled. *What does Danielle know? She isn't his mother.*

At the nursing station, where a nurse was typing on a computer, Ellie leaned forward on her elbows. "Simon Webster's father is here," she said. "He'd like to talk to the doctor."

The nursed glanced at her. "Doctor will talk to you as soon as he can."

"Is my son okay?"

"You'll have to wait for the doctor."

A door opened. The bearded man in green pajamas approached. "I'm Dr. Karnes," he said to Nicky.

"Is my son all right?" Ellie stepped closer.

"The good news is that his pulse is up."

"Wonderful," Ellie said uncertainly.

The doctor sat across from them in one of the chrome-and-plastic chairs. "As you may know, Mr. Webster, we've pumped out his stomach and loaded him up with charcoal and a chemical to offset the effects of the Tylenol. It's too soon to know if his liver has been compromised."

"His liver?" Ellie stared at the doctor.

The doctor nodded slowly and glanced at his notes. "The tests take a few hours. I know the waiting is hard."

"Is liver damage reversible?" Nicky's tone frightened Ellie.

The doctor stroked his beard. "If there is liver damage — and there may not be — he could be very susceptible to toxic substances of any sort for the rest of his life. Any future use of drugs or alcohol could be dangerous."

"Why?" Ellie asked.

"The liver helps metabolize carbohydrates and proteins and fats and assists with the manufacture of red blood cells. You've only got one, so you want it to work well." The doctor's pager beeped shrilly. "Frankly, what concerns us more is hypoxia."

"Hypoxia?" Ellie held tight to her chair, staring at the picture on the wall of a sailboat heeling near Diamond Head.

Nicky opened his address book. "I think we should call Malcolm Collins." He turned to the doctor. "Malcolm's an internist at Stanford. We went to Yale together. I really think — "

"Nicky, shut up," Ellie hissed. "What's this hypoxia?"

"At some point before you found him, Mrs. Webster, he appears to have stopped breathing. His brain and his blood didn't get any oxygen. Probably not for long. But — "

"He'll be a vegetable? Is that what you're saying?"

Dr. Karnes shook his head. "At the moment all his signs are improving. There's no indication that — "

"But what about this hypoxia?"

"We've ordered an EEG. The techs will be up any minute."

Ellie could not bear it. Would she have two morons now?

"You can see him if you'd like, Mrs. Webster," said the doctor, pointing down the hallway.

They followed him past cubicles filled with IVs and tubes and machines and very sick people. Simon lay in the last room on the right. Her tiny sweet baby, whom she had fed and bathed and dressed and carpooled and loved for eighteen years, was lying in front of her in blue-polka-dot hospital pajamas, his face ashen, tubes fixed to his arms, his nose, and his mouth. The steady hum of machines whirred around them.

"Simon," Ellie whispered, kissing his forehead. "I love you. I love you very, very much." She bent lower. "I didn't mean what I said this morning."

Simon did not move.

"Ellie," Nicky said softly. "The doctor wants to know if we want a priest."

Ellie stared at him. "A priest?"

"In case he doesn't make it."

Ellie swallowed. "I don't want a priest." She turned to Simon, ghostly and pale. He looked so innocent, utterly incapable of throwing her into the kind of rage she'd felt this morning.

"Simon, please come back," she whispered. "Talk to me."

"Have you called your parents?" Nicky asked softly.

"No."

"They'll want to know."

"You call them."

There was only one person Ellie wanted to speak with now, and it was not her mother.

□ Part V □

Chapter 23

Kate's hand tightened on the receiver. Last night she had spoken to Ellie for the first time since their breakup. Ellie had been breezy, almost casual, inviting Kate to a barbecue for Simon's eighteenth birthday, apparently assuming Kate and she could resume their friendship as if nothing at all had happened. Today her voice was muffled and ghostly; she was speaking from the other side of the universe.

"Simon's had an accident." Last night she said he was great, the only member of his original rehab group who had not had a slip. "I found him in the barn."

"In the barn?" Kate's hands were shaking.

"He overdosed on Tylenol. He's unconscious."

Kate stared at the wall, at her portrait of Simon, finished now, in the crisis unit stooped over his Mickey Mouse notebook.

"Can you come down here?"

For six months Kate had survived on daily AA meetings, on phone calls with Stacey, on weekends spent with friends to avoid the long stretches of silence and solitude. She was almost human again. If she went to the hospital now, would she lose the peace of mind she'd managed to recover? "Will Alyson be there?" she said finally.

"I don't know where she is."

Ellie had seemed happy with Alyson last night, said they were looking at property in Santa Fe, didn't have the problems over sex that she and Kate had had. Today Ellie's tone was different. Kate took a deep breath. If she could help Simon somehow, do something for the family, wasn't that worth the risk? "What hospital?" she said finally.

"Menlo Park. On Turkey Run Road."

"I'll leave now."

Ellie was crying too hard to reply.

Kate was once again surprised by the deep blue of Ellie's eyes. They were wide and red from crying, her jaw tight, her hands shredding a Kleenex. Her skirt looked slept in. "His brain may not be working," Ellie said, embracing her. "I'll take you in."

She was not prepared for the sight of the tubes and catheters and wires connecting Simon's long body to machines and monitors and drips. Kate kissed his forehead, the only uncovered place on his body. He seemed unnaturally pale as the machines gurgled and hummed around him. The sight of his damp skin and scraggly beard filled Kate with memories — the tensions his presence had created in her relationship with Ellie, the admiration she'd felt for his honesty, his struggle against Thorazine and pot and insanity.

"Alyson's not here?" Kate asked. She dreaded the inevitable meeting.

Ellie continued to stare at her son. "I don't know where she is."

"Does she know what's happened?"

"I don't know."

Kate leaned against the wall. This was very strange. She was standing next to Ellie for the first time in months, with Simon unconscious, Nicky in the waiting room, Alyson in outer space. It was far from the romantic reunion she had envisioned as recently as last night.

"I can't tell if he's better or worse." Ellie sat on the edge of the bed, touching Simon's knee. Kate noticed that his chest, which was covered with a pale beige sheet, was moving up and down.

"I told Simon I wished he were dead." Ellie's eyes looked guiltily at Kate, who was surprised by the view from this room of the green ridges of Turkey Run, where she and Ellie had ridden that first moonlit evening two years ago.

"I was upset this morning." Ellie held her chin in her hand. "Because of your call."

It was your call, Kate wanted to say.

Simon coughed; one of his machines began to beep. Ellie dashed out to find a nurse.

"Just his IV." The nurse clipped off a tube and deftly replaced the old bag with a new one.

It's so natural and so unnatural, Kate thought, *to be here with Ellie. She looks so lovely, so much the same, with the same high cheekbones, the same shoulder-length brown hair. Even in this setting Ellie's physical presence makes my knees soft.*

"It's okay, isn't it, that I called you?" Ellie's eyes begged for Kate's approval. "You don't mind?"

"It's fine." Had Ellie been drinking? Was the smell of alcohol coming from her breath? Last night she'd said she was on the wagon.

Nurses came and went. Suddenly Nicky was shaking Kate's hand, telling them both that Ellie's parents would arrive at midnight. Mrs. Kwaznicky was taking care of Nathan. Johnny had been told. Ellie's friend Mary Jane, he said, was in Mendocino and would be down late tonight. This time Kate did not feel nervous with Nicky; he was simply someone who, like her, had once been desperately in love with Ellie.

"I'm starved," Ellie said suddenly. "I'll take Kate to the cafeteria." She took Kate's arm. "Can I bring you something, Nickers?"

"Turkey, if they have sandwiches. And a 7UP?" Nicky offered Ellie a twenty-dollar bill, which she flicked away. Both gestures made Kate sad.

The cafeteria was closed, but the vending machines worked. Kate bought two 7UPs, one for Nicky, one for herself. Ellie tore open a bag of Cheese Thrills with her teeth. "I have a favor to ask, Katie." They sat down at a long green table.

Kate's hands were cold. A young African-American woman was banging the vending machine. She had lost her quarters inside it. A hospital aide joined her in pounding the coin return.

"Come home with me tonight."

Kate stared at her.

"As a favor to me…and to Simon."

"Are you going home?"

"Eventually."

"What about Alyson?" Kate chewed her plastic straw.

"It's over with Alyson." Ellie leaned so close to Kate that her breast touched Kate's shoulder.

"Your parents will be here. They'll want to see you."

"I don't care what they want." Ellie leaned forward. In the fluorescent lights her face turned pale green. "They can stay in a hotel."

One last kick from the aide caused the vending machine to belch up a host of quarters. "Yes!" yelled the woman as the coins clinked out like a slot machine in Reno.

Ellie squeezed Kate's hand. "I'm not the same person I was, Katie. I've changed."

"You won't always feel this scared," Kate said quietly. "When's Simon's better, you'll — "

"I'm not scared," Ellie interrupted.

"Concerned then."

"I'd like to try again, Katie."

Ellie's arm around Kate's shoulder was turning Kate on. What the fuck was it about this woman? They were sitting in a hospital cafeteria with Simon unconscious and Ellie distraught, and Kate wanted to undress her right here. *Shit!* Kate was appalled by her body's betrayal. "Simon's going to be okay," she said slowly, the carbonation from the soda growling in her stomach. "He's very strong." He was breathing, after all.

"What about us?" Ellie moved closer.

Kate gulped. She had been in love with Ellie since she was fourteen years old. "I'll always love you," Kate said softly, moving away from Ellie's arm. "I'll never stop loving you."

Ellie kissed Kate's hand.

"But this is not the time to discuss our relationship."

Ellie tapped her cigarette ashes into the battered little aluminum ashtray on the table. "Katie, my son is up there dying."

"Maybe he's not. Maybe we should go back up and — "

"I'm not the person I was before."

Kate smiled. "I loved that person very much."

"Thank you, my sweet." Ellie inched closer. "I was callous and self-centered and scared of being a lesbian. I'm not that way anymore."

Kate thought of Stacey and Lucy and her friends in AA who'd spent months helping her regain her self-esteem, trying to persuade her how much better off she was without Ellie in her life. Would she throw all that out for one night with a crazed woman whose son had attempted suicide? "Shouldn't we get back to Simon?"

"I'll be making money in real estate soon," Ellie said, lighting another cigarette. "I'll kick the tenant out of the big house, and we can live there together, where there's space. And the guest cottage will be your studio as we'd always planned. We'll be a family and grow old together as we said we would."

Amazingly the picture Ellie painted appealed to Kate. But just last night Ellie had been happy with her life. How could she, in — Kate glanced at her watch — less than twenty-four hours drop Alyson and decide to make a new life with Kate?

"I know what I'm doing," Ellie said. "I figured it out this morning before I found Simon."

"Mrs. Webster?" A nurse from the ICU called from the doorway.

Ellie ran to the door.

"Follow me, please."

Kate chased after them with Nicky's 7UP, up the stairs and down the long hall and into the small cubicle where Simon lay, Nicky sitting next to him. His eyes were open. The tube had been taken from his mouth.

"Sweetheart!" Ellie fell to her knees and kissed his hand. "Oh, sweetheart. You're awake."

Simon's lips moved, but no words came out.

Ellie leaned closer. "I love you, sweetheart. I love you very, very much." Ellie wiped her eyes.

A small frown tightened Simon's face. "I fucked up."

"No you didn't, my love." Ellie's cheeks flushed with pleasure.

Simon stared at her. "Love you, Mom."

"Oh, my sweet, I love you too. You're going to be okay."

Ellie turned to Kate, tears streaking her cheeks. "Talk to him, Katie. Tell him how much I love him. Tell him how much everybody loves him. You and his dad and me and Johnny and…"

Kate stepped forward and touched his arm. "Hey, Si."

Simon coughed, a long, bubbly cough, and closed his eyes.

"What's wrong? What's happened?" Ellie rang frantically for the nurse.

Simon opened his eyes. "I'm okay, Mom," Then he closed his eyes and fell back to sleep.

At 1 A.M. Kate left the waiting room and walked into the hall. Ellie followed her. "Will you come home with me tonight?"

"You won't be going home tonight."

Ellie took Kate's hand. "Why won't you?"

Kate looked down at her feet. "You have a life with Alyson now."

"If she's there, I'll tell her to go home." Ellie pulled Kate to her.

Kate was again amazed by her own desire, shocked that she could feel so turned on by Ellie after all that had happened, with Simon laboring in the room nearby. She wanted to say what she hadn't said last night when Ellie had called. "We made each other up," Kate began. "We're neither one of us what we seem. We weren't then, and we aren't now."

Ellie looked puzzled. The elevator bell chimed as it opened. "I didn't make you up. I know you as well as I know myself. I've known you for twenty years."

Kate lifted her backpack over her shoulder. "You believed I was strong and self-sufficient and could get you out of your marriage without needing too much from you."

"That's not true."

"And I believed..." Kate felt the tears.

Ellie waited.

Kate reached for the railing. "I believed that your love could make up for all those years when I had no one to talk to and parents who thought that being queer was sick. When I lost it again, it nearly killed me."

"You've never lost it." Ellie's hands gripped Kate's elbows.

As Kate was about to speak, a young man with hollow cheeks and huge, desperate eyes, his face spotted with dark red lesions, shuffled past them clutching his IV pole. Kate looked away. "We couldn't see what was in front of us."

"Kate Paine, what I see in front of me is the woman I've loved since high school." Ellie's eyes grabbed Kate's. "What do you see? Are you disappointed that I'm not the goddess you thought I was? I told you that the first night we were together. We'll start again with open eyes."

The smell of alcohol still emanated from Ellie's body. "You're a beautiful woman, Ellie. But you use people to make yourself happy."

"You *made* me happy," Ellie cried, shaking Kate's arm.

"No, I didn't." Kate's grip tightened on the railing. "You were bored with me. Both times." The elevator door opened. A nurse in a green surgery gown hurried out.

211

"I was blind," Ellie said, holding Kate's arm.

"So was I." Kate swallowed tears. "I thought you really loved me."

"I do, Katie."

"No, you don't." Kate shook her head. "You love a fiction. You want a dream — a strong, successful artist with no self-doubts and plenty of money."

Ellie picked up both Kate's hands. "I've made mistakes. But I've changed."

"You hadn't changed last night," Kate said, fighting her anger. "Last night you loved Alyson."

"I see what's important now." She glanced behind her at the door to intensive care.

"For how long?"

"Katie, I was raised to lie. My father's a spy who still swears he only sold sewer pipes to Third World countries. My mother's a Jew who's convinced herself she's descended from a long line of Episcopalians. I've got a lot to learn, Kate. I know that. I don't want to lie and hurt and throw away the people I love. We'll do it together this time."

The elevator door opened again. Kate did not move. She was having the conversation she had wanted for a lifetime. "Let's talk about this another time."

Ellie chewed her lip. "I'll go to therapy. I'll do whatever you ask."

Kate smiled. "Take care of your son."

Ellie frowned. "I've been doing that for eighteen years."

Kate smiled. A woman's voice over the loudspeaker paged one of Simon's doctors. "You didn't see the goddess in me, Ellie."

A cry emanated from Ellie's chest. "I *did*. I *do* see her, Katie," she whispered. "But you don't see the goddess in yourself. And what can I do about that?"

Kate cocked her head to one side, confused. Was it true? Had the problems between them been caused or somehow magnified by her own lack of confidence, by her inability to accept Ellie's love? Were Ellie's secrecy and her need for seduction somehow the result of Kate's insecurity? Kate hesitated. *Lucy,* she thought. *Ellie made love with Lucy the first month we were together.*

"You can't do anything," Kate said at last. She turned toward Ellie, kissed her cheek, and then slid to her right to the elevator. "I'll pray for Simon. I'll pray for both of you."

Ellie tightened her grip on Kate's hand. "Don't run, Katie."

"I'm not running." The elevator opened, and Kate stepped in. "I'm going home."

Highway 280 was empty, the sky black, a few pale lights blinking in the west on the far ridge above Turkey Run. Gratefully Kate inhaled the sweet smell of hay and sage and horses. She turned on the radio and heard a single violin playing Bach's Cantata No. 78, the two women singing sweetly, ecstatically. Simon Webster was alive, and Ellie, who had told her son she wished him dead, had asked her to come back.

She was glad to be driving away, heading north, leaving behind the Websters to their dramas and heartaches and intriguing passions. Perhaps life would turn out well for all of them. Ellie and Nicky would finally realize how precious Simon was to them. And Kate would at last *get* it — that Ellie Sereno's love could not fix her, could not ensure her confidence and self-esteem. That was an inside job.

In the morning she would call Stacey, then Lucy. There was so much to tell them both. Later in the day she would borrow her landlord's scull and row out to the palm tree island. From there she would look back at the hills of Sausalito and begin a landscape, not a portrait, in which all that could be seen of her life and her loving was a dark spot, a roof amid the green ridge of trees above the water.